THE FUTURE SCROLLS

'You have much to bear for an honest man...'

Alexander Mendeneres' family have had a set of scrolls ever since 1200 AD, when a heavenly messenger chose a scribe to record the gods' predictions for mankind. Now Alexander's wife has stolen the priceless articles and taken them to the United States to find a buyer and Alexander must use his young daughter as bait to trap his conniving spouse...

THE FUTURE SCROLLS

*Recent titles by Fern Michaels
from Severn House Large Print*

PICTURE PERFECT
SPLIT SECOND

THE FUTURE SCROLLS

Fern Michaels

Severn House Large Print
London & New York

This first large print edition published in Great Britain 2002 by
SEVERN HOUSE LARGE PRINT BOOKS LTD of
9-15, High Street, Sutton, Surrey, SM1 1DF.
First world regular print edition published 2001 by
Severn House Publishers, London and New York.
This first large print edition published in the USA 2002 by
SEVERN HOUSE PUBLISHERS INC., of
595 Madison Avenue, New York, NY 10022

British Library Cataloguing in Publication Data

Michaels, Fern
    Future scrolls - Large print ed.
    1.   Romantic suspense novels
    2.   Large type books
    I.   Title
    813. 5 ' 4 [F]

    ISBN 0-7278-7145-5

Printed and bound in Great Britain by
MPG Books Ltd, Bodmin, Cornwall.

Prologue

AD 1200

I write in this journal for the benefit of Alexander Mendeneres – my friend, confidant and physician. I believe this will ease my soul and free my mind. I have great confidence in my learned physician's opinions, but I fear I shall not live much longer once this journal has been finished. The mark of death is upon me. I pray that God will give my hands the strength to finish these last passages.

It was while I was kneeling for evening devotions that the miracle – for I am convinced it was a miracle – happened.

As I prayed, I became aware of a disturbance in the calmness of my room. The very air seemed to buzz with energy. The buzzing became louder, causing the air about me to stir and creating a gentle breeze. As it became stronger, I experienced the winds of a hurricane flinging my bedclothes around the room and forcing my prayer book to fly to the other side of the chamber.

Frightened, I closed my eyes tightly, willing whatever it was to leave me in peace. But, through the thin skin of my eyelids, I sensed a light so bright that when I tried to open my eyes I was nearly blinded with its brilliance. Now I became truly frightened, for it was late evening and I realized that no candle could ever have accounted for the intensity of light that I was witnessing.

I cautiously looked about me, and, there, standing by my bedstead I saw a figure of a man, but I knew no earthly creature could ever be as beautiful, as beatific as he could. He was tall, with skin pale as the wings of a moth and the blush of peach. Golden hair tumbled about his perfectly formed head, and he was beardless. His profile and features were refined, reminding me of a painting of an ethereal being. A smile of empathy radiated from his face. He was well-proportioned and muscular, which the large, loose cut neck of his white robe, with trimmings in blue, enabled me to see. He wore no sandals and his feet were long and slim.

But most remarkable of all was the light which emanated from him. It encircled him like a halo, throwing its beams into the far corners of my chamber.

I drew back in fear and astonishment as I heard my name called, yet I heard not a voice. Incredulous as I was, I knew this man was a messenger from God. He told me to be not afraid, that he had not come to harm me but to enlist my aid. Owing to the beauty of his personage, I knew beyond doubt that I had nothing to fear. He put me at my ease and spoke of heavenly things and everyday happenings. Things I knew of and things which were obscure to me. He told me, at last, the true nature of his business, yet cautioned me to tell no one until the nature of his business was completed. This I obeyed.

Throughout the time he spent with me, I became to him a scribe and diligently wrote down all he had to say. His messages were predictions of things to come. I found myself listening to his words as I wrote.

Among the predictions foretold – which I do not hesitate to put down here, for my brethren, the Prefects of the Church, have already made them known publicly at my trial – he spoke of the coming of a king who would separate Church and State; the discovery of a new land far across the seas; the downfall of a great nation of people in this new land; the mention of great and devastating wars which have yet to be fought; and much more, which to this day I do not understand. Nor do I understand why I was chosen to write of these prophecies, nor do I recognize what use these prophecies will be to man. I only know that

9

a heavenly messenger was sent down to earth and he chose me to be his scribe.

When he left, leaving me a blessing, he said something that I thought very strange at the time. He said I had helped him of my own free will, otherwise he would not have stayed with me. He told me he had exerted no influence on me and my decision to be his scribe had been my own. I had but to have objected or to have shown a display of non-faith in him and he would have left me as he had found me. His face saddened as he looked upon me, and he said simply, 'You have much to bear, for you are an honest man. The grace of God will be with you, but it will not change the events of things to come. Be brave and strong of heart, and reflect on the sufferings on Calvary.' Then he was gone.

I had rolled the last scroll and placed it on the table. I then fell on to my bedstead in exhaustion. When I awoke the next day, I thought I had imagined the whole incident. But when I rushed to the table, I saw the rolled scrolls there. Carefully, I opened one of the parchments. What I saw there left me amazed, as well as convinced that my experience had not been an illusory one. There set before me, in my own hand, were the words I had set down at the angel's direction. The passages were involved, requiring study and reflection, though what most impressed me were the illuminated drawings with which each scroll began. The color was vibrant, more so than any ink or paint I had hitherto known of, and my touch with the brush was delicate and commanding. I knew the work to be mine and yet it far surpassed anything I had ever done before or, for that matter, any work I could ever hope to do. There were seven scrolls in all, each bearing the mark of the illuminated letter – or cross – at the top. I sat down on the stool near the table and tried to decide what was best to do. It was clear that I could not keep these happenings to myself. But now, as I lie in this cold dungeon to which I have been committed as a raving lunatic, I wonder if perhaps it would have been better if I had kept the scrolls a secret.

Now there is naught to do but to entrust the scrolls to Doctore Alexander Mendeneres and pray to God that he will safeguard them till the time comes for them to be revealed.

One

The public address system was announcing the arrival of National's flight 344 from Los Angeles at gate West 22.

Dani Arnold sat in the plush terminal restaurant sipping a cup of Starbucks coffee as she concentrated on the view that the wide panoramic window afforded her of the runway.

To any observer, Dani Arnold would have appeared to be a young, attractive woman in her mid-twenties, well groomed and intelligent looking, confident and poised, like so many other thousands of Manhattan career girls.

Her facade of tranquility belied the hidden turmoil boiling within her, contradicted the well of tears which threatened to spring to the surface.

She was tired, more so than she could remember having felt for a long time. The strain of the past two hours was taking its toll and the caffeine in the coffee wasn't helping her to keep her emotions under control.

13

Wasn't it just like Jack to be callous enough to ask her to see him off to the airport, so he could wing his way to the 'girl back home' and his impending marriage? And wasn't it just like her to agree! Dani, old girl, she thought wryly, you weren't dealt a full deck. The minute you heard Jack's voice on the phone last night, you should have slammed down the receiver so hard that his brain would still be jingling now from the reverberation.

A jetliner began its slow progression down the runway in preparation for take-off, but her thoughts were still focused on Jack.

A feeling of defeat rivered through her as she thought about how she had built her hopes around him, trusted him with her most tender emotions and allowed him to see her vulnerability. Jerk that he was, and to use that trite phrase, he had wined and dined her into a deep, prolonged assurance that she would one day be Mrs Jack Cecil. No, that was all wrong – she was the jerk.

Then, one stormy, rainy night, when they were nestled cozily before her electric fireplace, he looked deeply into her eyes and said he knew that she would understand. He had decided to return to the 'girl he had left behind' in his home town, and couldn't Dani and he consider themselves 'good friends'?

The girl, Dani had come to find out, was

an heiress and Jack had found that life as a poor, struggling lawyer in the big city was not as attractive as being a poor, struggling lawyer in a small town with a rich wife. This revelation had taken place two months ago and she had not heard from Jack until the night before.

When she heard his voice on the phone, her traitorous heart had leaped and threatened to strangle her to the point where she had to choke out her words. But all Jack had wanted was for his 'good friend' to take him to the airport because he'd sold his car and it would be good to see Dani again.

Before she realized what she was saying, they had ended their conversation and Dani had agreed to borrow Stash's car and take Jack to the great, silver bird that would wing him all the way to his wedding.

Now with Jack gone from her life, although he assured her his business would bring him to New York and he would look her up (he had punctuated this with a wry wink), Dani felt hollow, emotionally depleted. Yet, priding herself on her logical New England thinking (discarding the fact that she had only spent a brief vacation at Cape Cod), she knew she would weather out this trauma and life would again hold new promise. The only cloud that darkened her sky was that she had no idea just how long this storm would last. She had not

15

gotten over him before last night, so maybe it was going to take forever? That's because I was still hoping, she derided herself. Now I know that anything I'd hope for would be after the fact and, besides, she grimaced, Jack is a dick! She dotted the expletive with a hard, sharp click of her cup against the saucer.

The waiter, hearing the clink of china against china, stepped over to her table and refilled her cup from the Pyrex pot that was always at hand.

Dani, not wanting a third coffee, smiled up at him, thanked him and resigned herself to another cup, not wanting to slight his well-intentioned attendance by refusing it. What was one more cup of coffee in the scheme of things?

The waiter, ever on the alert to the needs of his patrons, took his coffee pot to a table on the far side of the restaurant in order to refill the cup of a distinguished-looking gentleman in his late thirties.

The man was well dressed in meticulously tailored gray sharkskin, which offset the wisps of gray hair at his temples and contrasted handsomely with his coal black eyes. As he poured the coffee, the waiter was startled when he noticed that the man's hands were tightly clenched, contradicting their owner's nonchalant pose. So startled was he by the fierce grip that one of the man's sun-browned, square, neatly manicured hands had of the other that he almost poured the cup to overflowing.

The gentleman shook his head in thanks and gazed across the half-empty restaurant to the windows looking out on to the runway, his gaze passing quickly over Dani's neat, shining dark brown head.

How can I sit here drinking what these Americans pass off as coffee? I should be out there somewhere searching for her, calling her name. His breath caught in his throat as he mentally called upon the heavens to bring his child to him. Maria, he silently moaned, Maria. What happened to you? Where are you?

His anger was red hot as his mind roll-called the events of the past few hours. Spare me from the inefficiency of airline personnel, he thought, grasping his hands together into a tighter clench, how can a ten-year-old child traveling alone all the way from Argentina go unnoticed?

If only I could see her now, rushing through the heavy glass doors of the airport restaurant shouting out 'Papa' in her sweet melodious voice. Maria, Maria, where are you?

He had gone the rounds of the airline officials and now it was past noon and there was still no word of her, no news from anyone who might have seen her. He was

17

still waiting for personnel to check with staff whose shift had changed at seven in the morning. This was the only explanation they could offer him: Maria had somehow come to the United States on an earlier plane and this is why he couldn't find her. But why would *Madre* change the plans and send Maria on an entirely different flight from that which had been confirmed? It didn't make sense.

He had thought of calling his mother in Argentina and questioning her, but the *Senora* was advanced in years and suffering with crippling arthritis. To worry her with Maria's disappearance would be the height of cruelty. No, he resolved, I will only call *Madre* as a last resort.

Was it possible that Maria had run away, guessing at his intentions? He would do what he had to do; use his child as bait in this deadly game that his wife had initiated. When his quarry reached out, as she would, he would withdraw her and hold her close. He, Alexander Renaldo Mendeneres, would never be the loser in this hateful cloak-and-dagger game.

Abruptly, the man pushed his chair away from the table, stood and flung a crisp bill on to the pristine, white tablecloth then left the restaurant with long, angry strides.

His movements distracted Dani from her thoughts and reminded her that there was

18

much else she could do with a rare day off from the office besides sitting and watching planes bouncing along a runway.

Hastily, she gathered her gloves and handbag, withdrew a crumpled bill from her coat pocket and left the restaurant.

Once outside, she seemed to lose her determination to leave, and she stepped up the few steps on to the observation deck which on one side gave a glassy view of the runway and, on the other, a bird's-eye view of the reception room reserved for VIPs. Without knowing why, her attention was drawn to a dark-haired woman wearing a tan cashmere coat with an enormous fox collar. The woman was engaged in conversation with a rather tall, thin man who had sandy-colored hair and a gold hoop piercing his right ear lobe. Both seemed tense and the man's eyes kept darting from the entrance of the room to its corners, as though looking for an escape route. The glamorous woman he was with also noticed his actions and put a comforting hand on his arm. Her soft, musical voice wafted up the bare walls reaching Dani, who was standing quietly, straining to hear the faint words. Even with the distance between them, she could hear every word they spoke, the woman now becoming angry.

'Eugene, try to control yourself,' she hissed. 'You're acting so suspiciously, you'll do something foolish, I know it!' She directed a further glance toward the doorway. 'You never could keep your head when it mattered most. I've passed through customs without a hitch – what are you worried about now?'

The man, resenting the woman's ridicule, took her arm in a vise-like grip and said hoarsely, 'Who could keep their head with a scatterbrained bitch like you to rely on? You may have cleared customs, sweet, but what about your airfreight?'

The venomous look on the woman's face would have chilled anyone else to the bone, but the man seemed impervious to her open hostility. She pulled her arm out of his vicious grip and laughed, a little tinkling laugh. 'Who's scatterbrained? Not I, Eugene. And I resent the bitch part, too. Don't ever say that to me again. For your information, they're not in the airfreight. They're right here, in my tote bag.'

The man's expression was incredulous, then, slowly, his upper lip curled into an evil smile. Dani watched his face change, as if in slow motion, from one of churlishness to one of mirth. His mouth spread into a wide grin and suddenly he exploded into laughter. His cackle, more than his boorishness, upset Dani. There was something abnormal in the way he completely surrendered himself to his jocularity. When he abruptly

20

stopped laughing, it was as though he'd never moved his lips at all, his features remaining cold and chiseled.

'Stop that insane laughter. Let's get out of here. I'm exhausted,' the woman complained in a whining voice. 'I never should have told Alex I'd meet him in New York. I never should have listened to you. Los Angeles is the place we should have designated. It's too cold here!'

'Shut up, will you? It has to be New York. I don't have the kind of contacts on the coast I have here. Now just shut up!'

The woman tossed him a disgusted look. Somehow Dani knew their argument would not stop here. It would probably be ongoing. It didn't sound to her like the two ever stopped arguing. It was none of her business, though. Why was she even listening?

'Lou and I were on the case all morning, and do you know what we were chasing? That brat of yours.'

'Maria?' The word exploded from the woman's mouth like a gunshot.

'Even you know she's a brat, Val. For five dollars I intercepted a cable addressed to Alex. It was from your mother-in-law. And what do you think was in the cable? It was the flight number and arrival time of the plane that kid of yours was on. It seems there was a little change in plans.'

21

Valerie turned to face him, a questioning look in her eyes. A smirk raised a corner of the man's mouth as he grabbed his companion's elbow and led her out of the VIP lounge.

Dani flushed. Suddenly she felt like a sneak for listening to the couple's conversation.

As the room emptied out, Dani was reminded of her determination to accomplish something worthwhile this day. 'Like take my library books back to the library,' she muttered.

Strong gusts of wind blew Dani's hair across her face as she sat on a bench outside the United Nations. What the hell was she doing here acting like some adolescent schoolgirl who'd just been dumped by the captain of the football team? Life would go on. So would she.

A tear forced itself from the corner of her left eye and rolled down her cheek. She wiped it with the back of her hand and looked up at the sound of the sharp rat-a-tat of the multi-colored flags as they whipped in the wind.

Feeling sorry for herself wasn't going to help matters and it was starting to get dark. She was a long way from her snug apartment. At least there she could always lick her wounds. Still, she hesitated. She felt the need to stay outside in the cool, bracing air. She knew she should go home. She wanted to go home. She belonged at home. Still, she didn't move. Instead, she reached into her bag and fished around for a crumpled pack of cigarettes. One cigarette while she let her mind loose. She had to pull everything out in the open and look at it. She held the small butane lighter close to the cigarette, the wind almost extinguishing the hardy flame.

Dani dragged deeply on the cigarette as she watched a small girl on the opposite bench. A picture-pretty child. She looked as Dani felt. It was almost dark. The girl should be home safe behind closed doors. What in the world was she doing here? Dani frowned. Another ten minutes and it would be completely dark. She watched as the child rubbed her eyes with the back of her hand, just as Dani herself had done minutes ago.

Dani looked around, not a soul in sight. Not even a policeman. The child's mother must be worried sick.

Don't get involved. What did that mean exactly? Don't care about the next person. Do your thing and let the rest hang loose. She sighed. Well it wasn't the way she did things. She always got involved one way or the other. A weary smile played around the corners of her mouth. What was it her father had always said? That tired old trite saying,

'Do unto others as you would have them do unto you.' She tried. And for the most part it worked. Her father had always said, 'Your mother and I did the best we could for you and your brother, now the rest is up to you. Use your common sense and heed advice, but make your own decisions. Keep your morals intact and hope and pray that the next person is doing the same.' How many times those words had come to haunt her. Living in New York wasn't the easiest place in the world to live. She had to compromise so many times. However, she sighed wearily, she had done the best she could, of that she was sure. Oh, there were times when she had to beat her breast in frustration and anger but, in the end, as her father said it would, her common sense had won out.

I am a good person, she murmured, defending her thoughts. I know I am. So I will get involved. I have to, that's part of my belief. Shades of the Good Samaritan straight from Sunday school. I've gotten my fingers burned before, but that's the chance I'll have to take. It's what I believe in.

Dani walked over to the child and looked down at her. 'Can I help you?' she asked softly. There was no reply.

'Are you lost? Would you like me to take you home?'

No reply. The little girl looked up and stared at Dani. There was fear and dislike in

24

the child's eyes. Something else, what was it? Dani thought. It was gone so quickly she could not put a name to it.

She sat down on the bench next to her. 'Did you by any chance run away from home?' she asked in a conversational tone. 'If so, I expect there are scads of policemen just waiting to take you home.' Still no reply. 'Would you like to have me drop you off someplace? I plan to take a taxi home. Come,' she said taking hold of the bright plaid sleeve of the girl's coat.

The young girl jerked her arm away so fast one would have thought Dani's gentle touch was a wasp sting. Obviously the child had been taught not to trust strangers.

'Well if that is the way you feel about it, then I suppose you'd better stay,' Dani said gently. 'I only wanted to help you. I have to leave now. You see I have a most demanding friend who is right this minute at home waiting for me to serve him his dinner and if he doesn't eat on time he gets quite impatient with me. There's no telling what I'll find when I get home,' Dani confided in mock horror. 'Why, this time I wouldn't be surprised if he slinks into the bathroom and knocks over my expensive bottle of Avocado Bath Oil and laps it all up!'

At the child's look of disbelief, Dani laughed and explained, 'My permanent guest for dinner is a most remarkable and, I

25

might add, very elegant cat named Bismarck. You can come if you want to. If not, then stay here. Goodbye whatever your name is.' Quickly, Dani stood and started to walk away. Presently she looked down at her side and saw the young girl, her black patent leather shoes making tapping sounds on the hard concrete. Dani looked at the shiny shoes and the white knee socks in the dim street lighting and thought that she hadn't seen a child dressed so well in a long time. All the kids today wore blue jeans and ratty sneakers. She wondered where the girl came from.

Dani hailed the first taxi she saw and she and the child climbed in. Having given her address to the driver, Dani leaned back against the hard seat. She eyed the steel grill that separated her and the child from the driver. She whispered to the little girl, 'I wouldn't drive a cab in New York if they paid me diamonds at the end of the day.' She'd had enough of city traffic when she returned Stash's car that afternoon on the way back from the airport.

Maybe taking the girl wasn't such a good idea. Good Lord, what am I going to do with her? Should I take her to the nearest precinct? Or should I ask her for her parents' phone number and give them a call? I can phone them and they can come and pick her up. That's what I'll do, I'll

26

contact them as soon as I get home. She risked a glance at the tired, tight-lipped girl perched on the edge of the seat next to her.

The cab made excellent progress across town and they were home before she knew it. Once she had paid the driver, she helped the youngster from the cab. 'Come on, I live here,' Dani said, pointing to a large building.

Two

As Dani switched on the lamp by the front door, she noticed the little girl's nervousness. She watched as the child's gaze swept around the room. When she saw nothing to frighten her, she let out a sigh. As yet the youngster hadn't uttered her first word.

'You can hang your coat here,' Dani said, opening a closet door. She watched as the child carefully unfastened a row of shiny buttons and removed her coat. Meticulously. She took off her matching hat and stuck it in the sleeve of the coat. Her task completed, she stood back, her arms folded in front of her. Dani looked at the glen-plaid pleated skirt and the soft beige cashmere sweater with the Peter Pan collar. While her dress was neat, it was dated, and Dani wondered if it was a uniform of sorts. Nowadays, kids wouldn't be caught dead in a similar outfit. Dani estimated her age at ten or eleven. 'Come on, I bet you're as hungry as I am. I make pretty good scrambled eggs, even if I do say so myself.' The little girl followed Dani and then sat down at the yellow and white table. Out of nowhere, a large tomcat leaped into the kitchen and proceeded to mew its delight at the sight of his mistress.

'Hi, Bismarck,' Dani said as she opened the door of the refrigerator. 'I know, it's chow time.'

At the sound of her voice, Bismarck started to purr so loudly that Dani laughed. She watched as he tiptoed daintily to the refrigerator and sat back on his haunches. He favored his mistress with a woeful, hurry-up-and-feed-me look.

Seeing that his meal was in progress, the old tom licked his whiskers and looked around the bright kitchen. With one leap, he pounced on the child's lap. With a lot of squirming and jostling, he settled himself, much to her delight. Dani laughed. 'I see he's found himself a soft spot. He loves to be held, he's worse than a baby,' she explained to the little girl.

Hurriedly, she spooned cat food into a small dish and set a matching bowl of milk on the floor. Next she opened some soup and poured it into a saucepan. Dani beat the eggs and within minutes she had a light, tempting supper before the child. The girl ate greedily, never raising her eyes. She finished everything on the plate, and the last drop of soup in the bowl. Dani handed her a tall glass of milk and a thick slice of pound cake. She finished both the milk and the cake. Evidently, the child hadn't eaten for some time. Bismarck sniffed disdainfully when no crumbs dropped at his feet.

Dani leaned back and lit a cigarette. 'Look, I don't mind being a Good Samaritan and bringing you home and feeding you. I don't even mind you playing with my cat, but I have to take you home. Now come on, where do you live? If you don't tell me, I'll have to call the police. Now what's it going to be? If there's one thing I don't need right now it's a kidnapping charge. Do you understand what I'm saying?'

The child looked at Dani. Her large brown eyes pleading. Dani, inexperienced as she was with children, didn't know what to make of it. 'Look, you have to tell me. Otherwise how can I help you. I will help, you know. Wouldn't you like to be friends?' she wheedled. 'No, huh? Well I thought you were too smart for that. Now I'm going to ask you one more time, then I call the cops and you get a ride and a free ice-cream cone. One more time, where do you live?'

'Brooklyn,' came the curt reply.

'Brooklyn!' Dani looked at the young girl with shrewd eyes. 'No you don't. Now let's try it again. Where do you live?'

'The Bronx,' the girl answered, hopefully.

'Let's try Park Avenue around 75th Street. How does that fit for size?'

The little girl looked puzzled and seemed jittery. She kept fidgeting on the small kitchen chair as she stroked the gray and black tomcat.

Quickly Dani reached for and grabbed the small patent leather handbag that rested on the shiny tabletop. The child screeched as the cat jumped from her lap.

'That is mine. Do not dare to open it. It is my personal property,' she said in precise, stilted English.

'Oho! So the cat does have a tongue,' Dani laughed. 'What's in this little bag that makes you afraid to have me look in it? I know, you're a secret hashish smuggler and you have a secret coded map sewn in the lining,' Dani giggled, trying to put her guest at ease.

A smile tugged at the corner of the young girl's mouth. So she was human. Dani continued, 'I am well aware of the fact that this is your personal property and I won't open it if you level with me.'

'What is that "level"?' the child asked, puzzled.

'That means, to tell the truth. By the way, I really think it's time we introduced ourselves. I'm Danielle Arnold, Dani for short, and I originally come from Brooklyn,' she said, extending her hand.

Solemnly, the child said, 'I am most happy to make your acquaintance, Danielle Arnold

31

from Brooklyn. I am Maria Elena Magdalene Mendeneres, the daughter of Alexander Renaldo Mendeneres, and I am from South America, newly arrived in this country today. I am also afraid that I am lost. There was no one at the airport to meet me. My luggage appears to have become lost and I have no money. I wonder if you would be so kind as to, how you say,' she frowned, 'put me up.'

'Uh huh, yeah, well ... Is that the truth?'

'But of course,' Maria said seriously. 'I do not lie. My papa would be very angry if I were to make a lie.' When she said 'papa', the accent rested on the last syllable.

'He would, huh? Well just where is this papa of yours that he lets you run around the streets of the wickedest city in the world?'

'I do not know! There was no one to meet me at the airport. I had to go through the customs myself. You see I had a ticket pinned to my coat. Just like a refugee,' she said proudly.

'Where is this ticket?'

'It blew away in the wind,' Maria replied.

'I'll just bet! What's in this handbag that you don't want me to see?' Dani asked as she handed the shiny black purse back to Maria Elena Magdalene Mendeneres.

'Only my passport and my handkerchief. You can see I am quite destitute,' the young child said, trying to suppress a smile. 'My papa will reward you handsomely for caring for me,' she said seriously. 'You do have money to care for me, do you not?' she asked anxiously.

'Well I might have a few stray pesos lying around,' Dani grinned. 'But I do work for a living. Unfortunately I don't have a rich papa. That is how one gets pesos here in New York. It's called hard work, honey.'

'I will deliver newspapers,' Maria said dramatically, 'to help buy food. You can have your chauffeur drive me to the people who will buy these papers.'

'I don't think that will be necessary,' Dani said, smothering a laugh. 'I have enough money to feed you for a few days until we find your papa. Do you know where your father is staying?' The child shook her head. 'Well, do you know what he is doing here in New York? Does he work here?'

Again, Maria shook her head. 'All I know is that he has most important business here. He made arrangements with my grand-mother to send me here. Papa wanted me to see the United States. It is my birthday gift. We had plans to see New York and the world of Disney in Florida. My grandmother sent a telegram to my papa, telling him that I was coming here with a note pinned to my coat.'

'Where is your mother, Maria?'

'I have no mother. Only my papa. My

mother was very beautiful and she came from the United States.'

Tactfully, Dani changed the subject.

'You said you had luggage. What happened to it? And don't tell me you don't know either. Let's start out on the right foot, Maria. If you don't lie to me, I won't lie to you.'

'My grandmother checked the airline and found a more direct flight for me to take. I was there when she sent papa the message.' Tears glistened in her eyes. 'I don't know why papa did not meet me. When I left customs and saw there was no one to meet me, I decided to take the limousine to the United Nations. I thought someone there would help me. When I tried to get out of the limousine, the man demanded money. I did not have any to give him, so he would not give me my luggage. And,' she said fearfully, 'he said he was going to call the police, so I ran into the building and hid in the bathroom *for hours*.' She spoke pitifully, as she watched Dani to see her reaction.

'Maria, what made you go to the UN?'

'I did not know where else to go. The United Nations is supposed to help all nations and all people. I come from Argentina. I thought they would help me.'

'Did you ask anyone for help?' Dani asked puzzled.

34

'Not exactly. You see,' she explained, 'when I finished with the customs and saw there was no one to meet me, I took the car. I guess I should not have done that. I thought the fare was included with my plane ticket. My money is in my suitcase, twenty-seven dollars thirty-three cents,' she added proudly. 'I do not usually have to worry about such things. That's when my problems started.'

'Hmm. How long were you sitting on that bench before I got there?'

'Oh, hours, and I was so hungry!'

Dani crushed out her burning cigarette and looked at the pixie face opposite her. Maria had beautiful olive coloring, rosy cheeks, large dark eyes – correct that, two intelligent brown eyes – and small, even teeth. She was going to be a handful, that was a given. Dani also had the feeling that the child was not telling her something.

Suddenly, the young girl blurted, 'I was afraid of those two men.'

'What two men? I didn't see a soul the whole time I was sitting on that bench.'

'How could you tell? You were crying, so you did not see me at first. Do you have the unrequited love affair?'

'You're something, do you know that? How old did you say you were? And not that it's any of your business about my love affair, unrequited or not.' Dani quickly lit another cigarette to cover her confusion.

'I am ten and one half, and you should not smoke so much. My papa says it is not good for you.'

'And what other little gems has your father spoken of?' Dani was annoyed. She knew she smoked too much and had been trying to cut down. Her ultimate goal was to quit entirely.

'My father is a very smart man. He almost runs the country single handedly.'

'Good for him. I bet he doesn't smoke either, right?'

'Actually, he does smoke but in moderation,' was the serious response. 'That is the problem with vices, did you know that? They are not bad if they are made in moderation.'

'Is that another one of papa's idioms?' Dani shot back sarcastically.

Maria nodded.

'I don't like your papa already. He sounds like a frightful bore. However did he get a child like you?'

'I am a love child,' Maria replied innocently. 'I was germinated right here in this wicked city.'

'Wha—?' Dani choked on the smoke she'd just inhaled. 'Don't tell me your papa told you that?'

'Oh, no. Grandmother told me.'

Dani coughed and snorted as she swallowed the last of her cold coffee.

'What time does the maid arrive?'

'Honey, while you stay here with me, you are going to be the maid. So get cracking and put the dishes in the sink. We'll do them in the morning. I don't have a maid. I'm only a poor working girl.'

'I can see that you are poor,' Maria said solicitously. 'I will see that my papa helps you when he arrives. You must have a maid and a chauffeur.'

'You know something, kid, you are absolutely right. Those are the two things I need most right now in my life.'

Carefully, Maria carried the dishes to the sink and emptied the overflowing ashtray.

'Now what shall we do?' Maria asked, friendliness personified.

'That's a good question. I really don't know too much about kids. What do you usually do after dinner?'

'My papa plays a game with me or we read together or he takes me for a drive.'

'Hmm. How about some television?'

'Oh, Danielle Arnold from the Brooklyn, I thought you would never ask! Can I watch some trash?'

'What?!'

'At home Papa will not allow me to watch the television. He says there is nothing but trash on the tube.'

'Well for once I agree with your papa.'

37

Dani laughed as she picked up the TV guide.

'Right now you don't have much of a choice. You can watch a *Seinfeld* rerun, the news, or *Walker Texas Ranger.*'

'Whatever,' the child said airily.

Once Maria was settled in the small tastefully furnished living-room, Dani beat a fast retreat into her bedroom. God, what was she going to do with this kid? Was she telling her the truth? She nodded to herself. The child just wasn't telling her all of the truth. In the morning she would call the airlines and make some inquiries and then she would call customs and, if need be, she would call the United Nations. It wouldn't be too much of a problem to take the day off. At least she would have a long weekend to decide what to do with Maria. Monday she would have to be back at work. Lighting another cigarette, she decided to close the drapes. As she looked out into the night, a lonely feeling washed over her. Dragging her thoughts away from things that could never be, she looked down into the quiet street. Across from her apartment building, two men posed nonchalantly in the doorway of the opposite building. Something in their manner appeared out of whack. One of the men looked pointedly upward. Inexplicably, Dani stepped behind the drapes. Too many old Bogart movies, she chided herself. Still,

38

she didn't reveal herself for a second glance, for at the back of her slim neck was the light, icy touch of fear.

Dani removed her knitted pants suit and slipped into a terry green robe. She smeared some cold cream on her face and tied her hair up in a knot on top of her head before she brushed her teeth and hung a week's worth of clothes back in the closet. Her tasks finished, she marched into the living-room. Maria looked at her in awe. 'Will you be beautiful when you are finished?'

'You can bet on it,' Dani answered sarcastically. She had to be smart, too, Dani sighed, shaking her head.

As Dani suffered through two additional hours of inane television, Maria basked in the light from the eleven-inch screen. The more stupid the program, the better she liked it.

Promptly at ten, Maria was sent into the bathroom and the set was turned off.

'There's an extra toothbrush in the medicine cabinet,' Dani called to the child's retreating back.

The sofa bed made up with extra blankets supplied from the stuffed linen closet, Dani fluffed up the pillows and sat down to wait. When Maria emerged from the bathroom, her hair was piled on the top of her head and her rosy cheeks were covered with a creamy white substance. 'Will it work for me?' she questioned. 'I would like to be beautiful when my papa sees me.'

'Honey, you are already beautiful. You don't need trappings,' Dani responded warmly to the solemn face.

'What is this "trappings"?' Maria asked curiously.

'Just some American slang,' Dani smiled, making a mental note to speak only the King's English to this strange child.

'I adore the American slang,' Maria said, bouncing on the sofa bed. 'My friend Anna and myself bought the American slang dictionary and the nuns confiscated it from us one night. But,' she added cheerfully, 'I did learn quite a lot first.'

'What did your papa think of that?' Dani asked dryly.

The girl's face clouded momentarily. 'He was not too happy. He wants me to grow to be the perfect lady.'

'Don't you want to be a lady?'

'Absolutely not! I have the wish to be the go-go-girl,' the child answered seriously. 'Do you know how to go-go, Miss Arnold?'

That should set Papa on his ear! Dani smiled to herself but answered soberly, 'I'm afraid not Maria. I lead, for the most part, a very dull life.'

The innocent guest looked crestfallen at her words, but perked up immediately. 'Then will you teach me to swear?' At her hostess' horrified look, she hastened to explain, 'I would not say the words out loud, Miss Arnold. I just want to know them in case of emergency.'

And that, Dani muttered to herself, should set Papa on his other ear. 'Actually, Maria, in this dull life I lead, I don't swear either. Sorry. Now come on, under the covers and I'll tuck you in. Tomorrow is going to be a busy day.' Quickly, she bent to straighten the covers and to give the child a quick peck on the soft, smooth, greasy cheek. Maria threw both arms around her neck in a stranglehold and gave her a smacking kiss on the lips.

'I think you will be the best friend ever, Miss Arnold, next to Anna,' she added loyally.

Dani gently disengaged herself from the child. She withdrew a tissue from her robe pocket and wiped Maria's cheek, forehead, nose and chin. 'Now you look truly beautiful,' she laughed. 'Go to sleep. I'll wake you in the morning.'

'Oh, I will sleep, Miss Arnold,' Maria sighed happily. 'The monk of Mendeneres will protect me ... and you, too, Miss Arnold.'

Three

Dani climbed wearily from her comfortable bed, feeling like she hadn't slept at all. Glancing in the mirror, she groaned. There were deep purple smudges above her cheekbones. Her heavily lashed eyes looked dull and lifeless. Trudging back into the small bathroom, she peered into the mirror again.

Maria poked her head around the corner of the door. Her small face registered shock at Dani's appearance. 'Perhaps later in the day it will work,' she comforted.

'What will work?' Dani snapped.

'That stuff you put on your face last night before you went to bed.'

'Go!' Dani shouted imperiously. 'Don't talk to me till ten in the morning. I'm a bear. Now scoot.' The child backed away from the door and scuttled to the unmade sofa bed. Eyes downcast, she sat with folded hands.

Mulling over the words of her new friend, Maria sighed. Why did it take older people so long to get together in the morning? She looked around the small living-room at the bright, colorful furniture, rich browns and deep tones of gold with bright orange pillows. Deep, comfortable chairs and a fireplace. Suddenly the phone pealed in the kitchen. Miss Arnold had closed the bathroom door, making it clear that she didn't want to be disturbed. Maria would have to answer it and take a message. She wouldn't interrupt that secret time in the bathroom a second time for the world. 'When I get older I certainly don't intend to glue and paste myself together in the morning,' she muttered to Bismarck as she marched into the kitchen. Bismarck added his agreement by curling up at her feet and purring contentedly.

'Hello,' she said softly

'Dani?'

'No, this is Maria. May I help you?' she asked cautiously.

'Maria, huh? Well now, that depends on what you had in mind,' came the deep-voiced reply. 'Is this 555-7732?'

'Just a moment, I have to look. Yes, you have the right number. Did you wish to speak to Miss Arnold?'

'Well now that I'm on the line it wouldn't be such a bad idea – that is, if it wouldn't be too much trouble,' the voice chuckled warmly.

'Well,' Maria hedged, 'it is not exactly convenient. Perhaps you would care to leave the message. I would see that she receives it as soon as she puts herself to ... What I mean is, I will see that she gets the message.'

The voice chortled. 'She's putting on her war paint, right? By the way, just out of curiosity, to whom am I speaking?'

'I am Maria Magdalene Mendeneres. And to whom am I speaking?' Maria asked coolly.

'I,' the voice replied huskily, 'am *Stanislaw Stashvitsky*. But you may call me Stash. All my friends do. If you're a friend of Dani's, then you're a friend of mine.'

'Thank you. And you may call me Maria. Now as to the message...'

'Never mind that message jazz, just bang on the door and tell Dani to get the lead out. I don't have all day. I have an establishment to run.'

'Ah, Mr Stash ... should I repeat the message exactly?' Maria asked in a jittery voice.

'Verbatim, kid. You'll be doing me a big favor if you hop to it right away. I have a lot of irons in the fire today.'

'Very good, Mr Stash. I shall attend to it immediately.'

Maria tiptoed into the bedroom and rapped softly on the bathroom door. 'I am sorry to disturb you, Miss Arnold,' Maria all but gurgled, 'but there is this ... this person on the telephone who says to deliver to you the message immediately.'

Dani opened the door and peered at the child standing in front of her. She didn't fail to see the dancing eyes and the merriment the little girl was trying to conceal. She waited.

'The message is...' Maria giggled, 'is to get the ... the lead out, he doesn't have all day and he has an ... establishment to run, and' – she groaned as she tried to stifle her laughter – 'he has irons in the fire.'

Dani smiled. 'Did he say his name was Stash?'

Maria nodded. 'And he has the most scrumptious voice. Is he your unrequited love?' she whispered conspiratorially.

Dani laughed. 'Afraid not honey. Just a very good, dear friend.'

Maria looked crestfallen. 'Does that mean he will be around to pick up the pieces? I read that once in a romance novel. Anna's older sister buys trashy books and Anna managed to sneak one to class.'

'No, that isn't what it means,' Dani said crossly. 'And stop worrying about my love life. Romance novels yet! Why aren't you reading *Goose Bumps* or *Nancy Drew*?'

'Love is so much more interesting,' Maria chirped, as she perched on the kitchen chair stroking Bismarck, who was nestling in her lap as though he belonged there.

'Hello, Stash, how are you?'

'Fine, and yourself. How's it hanging,

45

Dani old girl? Did the *Clarence Darrow* of tomorrow get off all right last night?'

'Yes,' Dani replied, her voice brittle. 'And thanks for the use of your car.'

'Anything for you, Dani, you know that. What say we take in a movie tonight? Dinner first of course. Bring your friend.'

'My friend happens to be all of "ten-and-one-half" years old.'

'So, I'm charitable. Bring her along.'

'Not tonight, Stash, but thanks for the offer. I will take a rain check, though.'

'Dani, how about something a little more definite? Like, when are you going to see all my sterling characteristics and realize I'm the only one for you? I'm yours, just ask me.'

'You are an outrageous flirt. One of these days I might take you up on the offer and then what would you do? Someday, you'll be standing in the right place at the right time and there, looking at you like you were the only man on this earth, will be the one for you.'

'Promise, promises,' Stash chuckled. 'OK, I just wanted to know if everything was OK. I have to buzz off now. I'll drop by in a day or so. Tell the kid I said goodbye.'

'Thanks, Stash. Stop in anytime.' Dani replaced the phone and watched Maria squirm on the chair, her head cocked at an angle.

Unable to control herself a moment longer, Maria asked excitedly. 'If he isn't your love, why isn't he? He sounded so...' – she searched for the right word – 'delicious!' she said triumphantly. 'Just delicious!'

'Actually. Delectable is a better adjective.'

'I adore the way he speaks,' Maria babbled. 'Shall I meet him? What kind of an establishment does he operate? And what exactly does "get the lead out" mean?'

'He runs a coffee shop of sorts. But he has a lot of sidelines. He has a boat he charters for fishing parties and, when he has nothing to do, he plays the guitar. And "get the lead out" means to hurry up. And before you ask, he looks like a Viking. He is also one of the nicest people in the whole world.'

'How magnificent. I cannot wait to see him. But,' she added loyally, 'there is no one as handsome as my papa. Women turn to stare at him all the time.' She watched Dani carefully, waiting for her reaction to this statement. She was disappointed. 'Perhaps you should consider this Stash as an alternative to your unhappy affair. What I mean is, you are unhappy, are you not? I saw you cry yesterday and there appears to be nothing around here to make you unhappy. Perhaps I may be of some assistance to you. In the romance Anna and I read, the lady did not sit by the phone waiting for it to ring. She went out and made it ring.'

'What?' Dani shrieked. 'What kind of story was that?'

'This lady went out and met all kinds of men and gave them her phone number and then they all started to call her. They called her a hooker. I think it had something to do with the number of phones she had in her house. She had so many calls that the first phone was always busy. But,' she added unhappily, 'I did not get to finish the story because Anna lost the book. Actually I think Carmen, a friend, took it when Anna wasn't looking.'

'I thought you said you went to a convent school,' Dani choked.

'I do,' Maria said happily. 'Oh I just love it here,' she said, dancing around the kitchen holding Bismarck in the crook of her arm. 'What shall I do to help, Miss Arnold?'

Dani sighed. 'Well, for starters, why don't you call me Dani? After all, anyone that sleeps on my sofa bed, wears my nightgown and eats my food, not to mention taking care of my cat and giving free advice to the lovelorn, should be allowed to address me as Dani.' She held out her hand and Maria offered hers, and both shook hands solemnly.

'Does this mean we are the good friends?' Maria asked, beside herself with happiness.

'Yep. Friends. You are now one of my best friends. So set the table. That's what friends are for.'

Dani removed a bag of frozen waffles from the refrigerator and popped them into the toaster. She poured blueberry syrup into a small saucepan and heated it. She then plugged in the electric percolator to prepare her caffeine fix for the day. 'Do you want milk or juice?'

'I'll have Pepsi Cola,' Maria responded.

'You'll have juice and like it,' Dani said, pouring a small glass.

Maria grimaced, but accepted the juice and the plate of steaming waffles. 'But this is very good,' she said, munching thoughtfully. 'You do very well without a maid.'

Dani grinned. 'It's a question of survival. I like to cook. This is nothing. I can whip up a gourmet meal in nothing flat. As a matter of fact, I intend to write a gourmet cookbook some day,' she said proudly.

Dani poured herself a steaming cup of the fragrant coffee and sat down. 'I think we need to decide what to do with you. Do you have any suggestions?' At Maria's negative nod, she continued. 'Then we had better start with the airport and your luggage. Next we'll go to the embassy. From there, if we have no luck, we'll send a cable to your grandmother. Does that meet with your approval?'

The child chewed industriously. 'Yes, Dani. I cannot imagine what happened to my papa. He must be very worried about me.'

'Why didn't you just wait at the airport? You could have had your father paged. Perhaps he was just late arriving at the airport.'

'But Dani, I did wait. For three hours I waited. Something must have happened to my papa. He would never have been three hours late. He is very punctual, and he demands punctuality of others,' she said seriously.

'Did you think to call the embassy yourself? Didn't your grandmother give you any instructions before you left?'

Maria shook her head. 'Grandmother was in bed with a severe attack of the rheumatism. Felix drove me to the airport and pinned the note to my coat. I felt like a baby,' she grimaced.

Dani smiled. 'I agree. You are a bit big to have a note pinned to your coat. I'm surprised that you didn't take it off.'

'I did,' Maria grinned in disgust. 'Actually, I removed it three times and three times I pinned it back on.'

'Come on. We'll leave the dishes and do them when we get home. Get your coat and I'll get my jacket. It's windy out.'

Bismarck watched as Dani and Maria slipped into their coats. He continued to glare at them, his long tail swishing furiously, knowing he was going to be left alone. Slowly, so as not to catch Dani's attention, he lazily stalked over to the door and stubbornly placed himself directly in their path. Through half-closed, yellow glittering eyes he measured their movements. Just as they were about to leave he stretched his long body across the threshold and closed his eyes tightly.

'Come on Maria, your hat looks fine. Let's get out of here before Bismarck notices.'

Maria ran to the door breathlessly, 'I'm ready, Dani.' Then seeing Bismarck, she fell to her knees, a worried frown pinching her pretty features. 'Oh, Bismarck, are you ill?' she asked soothingly. 'Does your stomach feel funny? Dani ... hurry, something is wrong with Bismarck!'

'Well, I guess you didn't hurry fast enough, Maria, the jig is up. Bismarck caught us getting ready to leave. You can't come with us, Bismarck,' Dani said sternly.

'You mean there is nothing wrong with Bismarck – he is just play-acting?' Maria questioned, a look of appreciation for Bismarck's talent evident in her face.

'I guess we'll just have to let him out, so he can visit his light o' love over on the vacant lot around the corner. Otherwise, we'll have a tug of war trying to pry all eighteen pounds of him out of our way.'

Upon hearing Dani's conviction that he

would be allowed to make his rounds that morning, Bismarck stretched, pulling himself to his feet as though waking from a sound sleep. Casting Dani a disdainful look, he waited for the apartment door to open and followed both girls out into the hall then waited, with them, for the elevator to take him to the ground floor. Once out on the street, they parted company, Maria with an exuberant wave of her arm, Bismarck with a quick flick of his bushy tail.

The ride to the airport was mixed with 'oohs' and 'aahs' on Maria's part. Dani leaned back against the seat and wondered what she was going to do with the child if she wasn't successful in locating 'Papa'. She had to return to work on Monday. Her job at the publishing house, where she was a junior editor, was a necessity if she wanted to survive. Besides, she knew if – when – she wrote a gourmet cookbook, she would stand a good chance of being published if she managed to stay employed in the industry.

'That will be seven dollars twenty-five, lady,' the cabbie said, breaking into her thoughts.

Dani paid the man and told him to keep the change.

The airport concourse was a beehive of activity. Everywhere she looked there were milling people, all in a hurry. The loud-speaker announced arrival and departure times. Redcaps trundled along pushing their dollies full of loaded baggage.

Dani grasped Maria's hand securely and bent down, 'Which airline did you arrive on, honey?'

'Transworld,' Maria answered quietly.

'Good, we'll start there.' Fifteen minutes later, standing in line, they knew no more than they had done when they started. 'We'll have to go to the baggage area. Let's hope that the limousine driver turned in your luggage. You have your half of the claim check, don't you?'

'No, a man took the check when I was given my luggage. But I will know it when I see it, Dani. It is bright red and my initials are on the handles.' Dani nodded as she weaved her way through the milling throngs of people. Arriving at the baggage area, she stood in line and waited her turn. She explained the situation to the plump, red-headed boy behind the counter. He shook his head 'no'.

'I don't understand. Didn't the limousine service turn it in? I mean, after all, she's only a child,' Dani said, more than a little annoyed.

'I can see that, Miss. But it's not here. There was a man here this morning asking about it. I looked for it then and it's not here.'

'Do you know who it was?' Dani asked.

'Not by name. He was a tall, distinguished gentleman, black hair and dark eyes. Dressed very well. That's all I can tell you.'

Dani looked down at Maria who was standing quietly by her side. 'Does it sound like anyone you know?'

'It sounds like my papa.'

'Terrific,' Dani said relieved. 'Now let's see if we can find the limousine service while we're still here and see if the driver knows anything.' Threading their way through the throngs of people, they made use of the stairs once more. Outside, they looked for the traditional long, black limousine. Seeing one standing by the entrance, they approached with much jostling on the part of the milling crowds.

Dani stuck her head in the window and spoke softly. The man in the dark blue livery touched his cap and waited. Briefly Dani explained the situation.

'Sure, Miss. That's the kid. I took her to the United Nations Building yesterday afternoon. Couldn't pay the bill. She had a bright red suitcase. I think she was lost, if you want my opinion.' Letting his eyes settle on Maria, he winked. 'No offense, kid. Now that the bill has been paid.'

'What? Who paid it?' Dani asked, surprised.

'Sure. Not more than half an hour ago. Some guy comes up and asks me real nice.

He even gave me a ten dollar tip.'

'Thanks a lot,' Dani said. 'Come on, Maria. I guess your father is on your trail. We won't be able to find him in this place, but as soon as he finds the cab driver that took us to my apartment last night, he'll rescue you.'

Maria nodded happily.

'In the meantime, would you like to see a little of New York? I don't have anything pressing to do today and I have a feeling it will take your papa a while to chase down that independent cab driver. Would you like to see the Statue of Liberty?' Maria nodded and smiled. 'Good. Then let's start there and then play it by ear.'

The next few hours passed happily, for Dani as well as Maria. They walked all day and only stopped once to gorge themselves on hot dogs and orange drinks. Dani bought the child a large, yellow balloon and a small music box that tinkled 'Raindrops Are Falling On My Head'. Maria was ecstatic over the gift.

At four o'clock, they sat on a bench in Central Park and removed their shoes. 'Did you have a nice time?' Dani asked conversationally.

'Oh, I had a lovely time, Dani. I want to thank you. It would only have been half as nice with Papa. He only takes me to places that will help me to learn. Then he gives me lectures on wherever we go. Sometimes it is very boring.'

'Tell me Maria, what is it your father does in your country?'

'He manages our estate. Did you know that Argentina is the market basket of the world? No? Well we live on what is called a *hacienda*. The land goes on for miles and miles in every direction. My papa, with the help of many overseers, runs the farm. We are landed gentry.' Dani favored her small charge with a dry smile. 'We have many servants to care for us. I have my own personal maid who takes care of me.'

'Well, you won't get that here, kid. Now, would you like to eat dinner at my apartment or have something to eat in one of the small restaurants nearby?'

'I prefer to eat at your apartment if it is agreeable with you. Perhaps we could dine while we watch television,' she smiled, looking at Dani hopefully.

'I think it can be arranged,' Dani laughed. They gathered their belongings together and walked to the exit of the park. Dani hailed a cab and within minutes they were back at the small apartment house that was Dani's home.

Maria immediately hung her coat in the closet and grabbed the tomcat that had been waiting in the lobby for them, and settled herself on the floor in front of the television. When Dani looked at the small happy face of the child and heard the contented purring of the cat, she felt a small tug at her heart,

'OK, Maria, I'll start dinner. If anyone comes to the door, don't you dare answer it. Call me.' Maria nodded solemnly.

Dani looked around the small, colorful kitchen she had worked so hard to decorate. It usually lifted her spirits, even if she was only making a cup of instant coffee. But now, for some reason, she couldn't get into the swing of things. She lit a cigarette and sat down at the bright, yellow table. Idly, she traced the ivy leaf on the place mats. She lit another cigarette and then another, only to crush them out. The tall, lovely girl felt like the sword of Damocles was hanging over her head. She needed to snap out of this funk and she needed to do it now. Allowing herself a mental shrug, she started opening and closing the kitchen cabinets. What to cook? Opening the freezer door, she scanned the shelves. Chicken Kiev. It would be quick. All she would have to do was heat the oil and make a salad. Next, she reached for the cherry cobbler she'd made one rainy Sunday afternoon. By the time the chicken was ready to come out of the oil the cobbler would have baked through. Briskly and efficiently, she set to work, her mind on her tasks.

As she set the table, she let her mind wander. How was Jack doing? Dani shrugged exaggeratedly as she took a long pull at the drink she held. So much for unrequited love! Lighting still another cigarette, she immediately crushed it out in the heavy, square earthenware ashtray that Stash had given her for her last birthday. She really did have to give up smoking. With one eye on the clock, Dani finished her drink. Tonight would be festive for Maria. She would use her best dishes – pure white ironstone – with large luscious strawberries in the center of them for desert. The matching napkins would add even more color to the table. After today she wouldn't see the youngster again, and she felt strangely sad at the thought.

Dani called Maria. 'Wash up, honey. Dinner is almost ready. Look, there isn't anything good on television except the news, so let's eat in the kitchen.'

'All right,' the child agreed. Gently, she placed the cat in his basket next to the refrigerator. She was back in minutes. 'How you say, a lick and a promise?' She grinned, holding out her hands for Dani to inspect them.

Dani looked at the proffered hands and nodded. 'Good enough. Sit down.' She served the golden chicken and salad to Maria before handing the girl a small oven-warm roll and filling her own plate. She watched the child cut into the tender piece of chicken and smiled at the expression on her face when the butter squirted out.

'Oh,' she squealed. 'My papa would adore this,' she said, biting into the Kiev. 'But it is delicious, Dani,' she said appreciatively.

'I'm glad you like it,' Dani said as she bit into her own perfectly cooked chicken.

'When do you think my papa will find me?' Maria asked between mouthfuls.

'Sometime tonight I would imagine. These independent cab drivers are hard to track down, you know. There was no point in my even trying – your papa seems to be on your trail. Are you so anxious to leave me, Maria?'

Instantly contrite, Maria gasped, 'But no, Dani. I shall hate to leave you, but I have not seen my papa for so long. I wish you lived with my papa, my grandmother and me. We would have such good times together. My papa will adore you.'

Dani drew in her breath. 'Don't count on it,' she half muttered under her breath. Somehow she knew that the father of Maria would not adore her in any way, shape, or form.

After dinner Maria politely offered to help with the dishes. Dani declined the offer, knowing the young girl wanted to watch a game show. The kitchen cleaned, Dani joined Maria in the living-room, gin and tonic in her hand. She lit a cigarette and watched two young boys answer questions to the tune of a loud drum roll, and Maria clapped her hands each time they gave the right answer.

The program over, Dani watched idly as Maria pressed the remote control's buttons that took her from one channel to the next. She looked at her watch and then at the phone. She felt her eyes stray from time to time towards the door, with its carved mahogany panels, that had so pleased her when she'd first moved into the tiny apartment.

While small, the apartment fitted her needs, away from the main stream of New York life. The plush, chocolate sofa was striking against the chrome and glass tables and matching etagere. The deep beige pile of the carpeting, with flecks of orange, contrasted with the mushroom-colored walls, flamboyantly picking up touches of color in the Chagall and Van Gogh prints in the room.

Her eyes traveled once more to the door. Who was she expecting – Jack, or Maria's father? Dani chain-smoked till after ten. Finally she looked at Maria. 'Come along, honey, I don't think your papa will be here till tomorrow. Let's get cleaned up. You can have the bathroom first. There's bath oil on the side of the tub. Towels are in the vanity under the sink.'

Dani switched off the television and picked up the evening paper. She scanned the headlines and moved on to the women's page. Looking at the gossip column, she noticed a picture of a striking-looking man. She read the caption: 'Handsome, wealthy Argentinian Alexander Renaldo Mendeneres dines at The Four Seasons with socialite Alicia Weverly.' Dani peered closer and gasped as she checked the date of the paper. Today's paper and today's date. 'Hmm. While I take care of his daughter, he nightclubs,' she snorted. 'Well, we'll just see about that. His daughter's lost and he's prancing around with women.'

Folding the paper carefully she laid it aside. God, what if she was wrong and he didn't show up for the little girl? What could she do? What would she do? She had already become fond of the youngster. She couldn't just leave her in some children's shelter. The child deserved better than that. Walking into the colorful kitchen, she decided to make another gin and tonic. Everything in moderation. Defiantly she lit another cigarette. Gulping at the tart drink, Dani flickered her fingers in the air. So there, Alexander Renaldo Mendeneres!

Dani marched back into the comfortable living-room, the cigarette hanging loosely from the corner of her mouth. Catching sight of her reflection in the foyer mirror, she quickly removed the cigarette from her mouth. Flopping dejectedly on the chair, she spilled half her drink. Back she went to the kitchen just as the phone shrilled. Standing still, she listened. Yep, it was the phone. Retracing her steps she picked up the push-button phone. 'Hello?'

'Dani? This is Helen. How about coming up to Connecticut tomorrow with Sue and me? There's to be a swinging cocktail party at Stacy's house to celebrate the sale of his latest book.'

Dani hedged. 'I'm not sure, Helen. Can I let you know tomorrow?'

Helen laughed. 'Are you trying to tell me you have a better offer?'

'You might say that,' Dani said as she looked at the shiny scrubbed-up girl in the floor-length nightgown standing in the bathroom doorway. 'If you don't hear from me by three, then go without me. And if I don't make it, have a good time and give my best wishes to Stacy. Anyone that can grind out those westerns with his speed deserves something.' Dani hung up the phone and looked at the child. 'My goodness, you look good enough to eat,' she laughed.

'I adore you, Dani,' Maria giggled as she threw her arms around her new friend. 'You always make me laugh.'

Dani smiled and hugged the child. 'Come on, let's fix your bed. Tomorrow is another day and I am sure your papa will be here in the morning.' Carefully, the young woman arranged the brightly colored sheets and the child climbed into bed.

'Tell me about New York, Dani, and all your friends before I go to sleep.'

'There isn't much to tell,' Dani said seriously. 'My mother and father were killed five years ago when they were taking a motor trip out West. I have a brother in the navy. He's stationed in Alaska. I have several aunts and uncles who live in Georgia. And that's all the family I have. After my parents were killed, my kid brother enlisted and I moved here from New Jersey and got a job, and this small apartment. This way when my brother gets a leave, he has someplace to stay. I still have my parents' home in Glen Garden. I haven't been back there since the funeral. I pay the taxes on the property and the neighbors watch out for vandals. I wish you could see the house, Maria. You would love it. It's a small Cape Cod home and has morning glories climbing all over the front porch. It has the biggest fieldstone fireplace that's just perfect for hanging your stocking on, on Christmas Eve. I have my job and lots of friends and for the most part I am kept pretty busy. Now tell me all about you.'

Maria sighed. 'I thought you would never

ask,' she giggled. 'Well, I told you I live with my grandmother and my papa and lots of servants. I have a very good friend. Her name is Anna. At the convent, the Mother Superior had to separate us. She said we were "thick as thieves". I got into much trouble. But I had a good time. That is important – to have a good time, is that not so, Dani?'

'Well, yes and no. First you have to learn, then you have a good time.'

'You sound like my papa,' Maria let out a loud cry of laughter.

Dani pretended horror at the declaration and, again, Maria laughed.

'I have a dog and three kittens. They are not half as pretty as Bismarck. I have the pedigree,' she said disdainfully. 'My grandmother is very indulgent and my papa is very strict but sometimes, how you say,' her brow furrowed in thought, 'I wrap him around my finger. I pretend that I have the bad stomach-ache and I cry. If that doesn't work, then I say that my head hurts. Usually, I win with the stomach-ache. Sometimes I have to use the headache, but not often.' She looked at Dani guilelessly, who found it hard not to smile.

'Now is that nice?' she asked.

'Probably not,' Maria said seriously, 'but then it is not nice to have secrets either. My grandmother and my papa have a secret. It has something to do with my mother. They will not tell me. I am old enough to know a secret. Do you think so, Dani?'

Talk about being put on the spot. 'It all depends. Perhaps it isn't a secret, just something that you aren't old enough to understand. Your grandmother and father are much older and possibly wiser than you. I'm sure that if it was something they felt you should know, your age would make no difference. Try to think of it in those terms.'

'Perhaps you are right,' the child said mollified.

'I think that's enough talk for now. We'll talk more in the morning.' Dani bent down to give the child a kiss and again found herself in an all-enveloping bear hug.

'I shall miss you, Dani, when I leave.'

'Honey, you know I think you're a very brave young lady. I know if I were your age I'd be afraid.'

'I'm not afraid, Dani. If you say Papa will find me, then he will. And I have you, and I know in my heart that you are good. Besides, the monk also protects me.'

'About this monk, Maria. What are you talking about?'

'The Mendeneres Monk!' Maria explained. 'It seems that I can teach you something, Dani. The monk has been dead many years,' Maria whispered conspiratorially.

'It's said that the first Alexander Mendeneres brought the monk's spirit to Argentina
hundreds of years ago. Grandmother said
our ancestor and the monk were great
friends. The monk has appointed himself a
guardian of the Mendeneres' family and
protects them from harm. Grandmother
tells me stories about the monk and they
make me tingle. I get goosebumps. But I'm
not afraid of the monk, Dani. He's good like
you are. But Mother is afraid. Whenever
Grandmother mentions him, Mother runs
to her room with a headache...'

Maria stopped her excited talk abruptly.
Aware that she had said more than she'd
planned.

'Your mother! But I thought she...'

Dani's words stuck in her throat when she
saw Maria's frozen expression and the hard
set of her round, dimpled chin.

Four

At times, she had forgone a lazy morning in bed after a hectic Saturday night. Somehow she found it easier to live with herself on a little less sleep without the remorse of having missed the Sunday service.

Dani woke with a start. She looked at the small bedside clock and jumped from bed. If she didn't want to be late for church, she would have to hurry. If there was one thing she did right, it was to go to church every Sunday. And on holidays, she added to herself. There were times when she couldn't find a Catholic church and she had gone to those of other denominations. What difference did it make, as long as one attended a religious service?

Twenty minutes later, Dani was ready for whatever the day would bring.

Opening her dresser drawer, she reached for her lace scarf and rosary. Dropping them into her tote bag, she quietly tiptoed back into the living-room so that she wouldn't wake the sleeping child.

But Maria was already awake. She sat on

the edge of the bed fully dressed, the paper opened to reveal the picture of her father. The youngster raised her eyes in mute appeal. Dani wanted to smash something. 'I'm going to church. Would you like to come? If so, get your coat. We'll have to hurry or we'll be late.' The child got up from the bed as if lead weights were tied to her feet She slipped into her coat and buttoned it with downcast eyes.

'I am ready.'

Dani held the door open, then quickly locked it before Bismarck realized she was leaving. The three-block walk to the Church of the Guardian Angels was made briskly, owing to the biting wind. Dani thought it appropriate that both she and the little girl should be going to the same church and no doubt thinking the same thing. We both need a guardian angel, she muttered under her breath.

Coming out of the tiny church fifty minutes later, Dani wondered if the dashing Alexander Renaldo Mendeneres would go to church. Probably not, she thought sourly. He was probably out on the town last night and would be nursing a hangover. Shocked at her thoughts after only just leaving the church, she prayed silently for forgiveness.

Dani and Maria walked to the crossing line at the nearest corner. While waiting for the light to change, Dani glanced behind her. Standing among the other parishioners were two men who appeared totally out of place. As the taller of the two turned to face her, she recognized the boorish man she had observed arguing with the elegantly dressed woman at the airport. Even at this distance, she could see the hooped earring piercing his ear. A chill of warning coursed through her, though she wasn't sure why. She reached for Maria's arm so quickly that the young girl gasped, alarm flickering in her dark eyes. The light changed to their favor. Dani hurried Maria across the street.

As they walked along, Dani realized that the two men at the church were the same two men who had been staring at her apartment window the first night Maria stayed with her.

Frightened, Dani put a protective arm around the little girl and rushed down the street towards home.

The child dragged her feet morosely and acted like she didn't want to return to the apartment.

'What would you like for breakfast this morning?' Dani asked cheerfully, trying to dispel the chills running up and down her spine. 'How about banana pancakes with fresh banana syrup? Or would you like Eggs Benedict? On the other hand, I can whip you up a hamburger with all the trimmings?' Getting no response to her monologue, Dani continued. 'If that doesn't tickle your fancy I can make you fatback and hominy grits.' Still no response. 'In that case, what do you say to both of us jumping off the bridge over there?' Pointing a long, scarlet-tipped finger, she said, 'You first.'

Maria looked at Dani in shocked amazement. 'Do you feel all right, Dani? Why should we jump off that bridge?'

'I have been talking to you for several minutes and you appear to be off in a world someplace else. Was it that picture of your father in the paper? Is that what's upset you?' Seeing Maria's stubborn-set face, Dani dropped the subject.

The moment they arrived at the apartment building, Maria scuffed her feet against the stone steps. 'Look, honey, we have to go in. I guess this is one of those things you will have to accept. If you want to be mature, you have to take all things that go with growing up, and understanding is one of them. Don't ever try to change something that you don't understand. Why not give your father a fighting chance?'

'OK, Dani, a fighting chance it is.' And she added imperiously, 'I will have the banana pancakes.' Her face broke into a gamin grin. Dani hugged the small child and together they entered the apartment.

Breakfast over, Dani poured herself a fourth cup of coffee. She looked at the kitchen clock: eleven twenty-three. He should be here by now. I'll give him till noon. If he isn't here by then, I'll call the embassy. The hands on the small, copper clock moved like two snails. At eleven forty-seven, the doorbell rang demandingly. Dani smoothed her long, chestnut hair and licked her lips. Slowly she walked to the door. She licked her dry lips again and quickly opened the door. God, he was a handsome brute. And right now he looked like a wild stallion held at bay.

'Miss Arnold?'

'Yes!'

'I am Alexander Renaldo Mendeneres. I have come for my daughter. Be so good as to fetch her immediately. In the future, it might be wise if you did not make a practice of abducting small children.' The voice was haughty and cutting, conflicting with the warm Latin accent.

'Just—'

'Maria!' the voice thundered. 'Come here immediately.'

Maria ran to her father and wrapped her arms around the tall man.

'Oh, Papa. I thought you would never come. I am so happy to see you. I have missed you.'

Dani watched the play of emotions as they flickered across his handsome, sun-bronzed face. At the sight of the child, the deep

71

trenches at the corners of his mouth softened. The smoldering eyes darkened with emotion as the child tightened her grip on his neck.

Dani was spellbound at the outpouring of love she witnessed between the man and his child.

'Have you been mistreated, Maria?' he demanded, concern softening the harsh edges of his tone.

'Oh no, Papa, I have had a good time.'

'Now wait just a damn—' Dani never got a chance to finish the sentence.

'You are lucky, Miss Arnold, that I do not press charges. In fact, you are most fortunate that I have a human side. How much ransom did you expect to get?' Not bothering to wait for a reply, he ordered Maria to get her coat.

'Just a "cotton pickin" minute, Mr Alexander Renaldo Mendeneres, I have—'

'Spare me your lies. I know your type. Come, Maria.'

'*My* type. And what is *my* type?' Dani sputtered. She looked into the ice-cold slate-colored eyes and shivered inwardly. 'On second thought, don't bother to tell me.' She made her own voice equally cold as she looked down at the small child and at the perplexed look on her face. 'Goodbye, Maria. Perhaps we shall meet again someday.' Holding out her hand to the child, she noticed the start of tears. 'You just hang in there little buddy and it will all work out.'

The child tore herself from her father's grasp and hugged Dani. Dani felt tears smart her eyes. Gently, she disengaged herself. 'Be good now and I'll see you around,' she said as if there were a frog in her throat.

With a last steely look that Dani returned in kind, the man ushered a tear-filled Maria through the door.

Dani looked at the closed door and suddenly ran to it and put the chain in place. Angrily, she raced from the kitchen. She made three gin and tonics and lined them up on the smooth, yellow and green counter top. Angrily she fished in the back of the cabinet drawer and brought out four ashtrays. Furiously, she lit four cigarettes, one after the other, and placed each of them in an ashtray.

Dani looked at the array in front of her and felt the tears trickle down her cheeks. Damn it to hell. What had she done? Not a thing. Finishing the first glass in three quick gulps, she reached for the first cigarette and puffed furiously. She then reached for the second glass. Taking a drink, she looked at the glass in her hand and poured the remainder down the drain. The contents of the third glass followed its mates. Crushing out the other cigarettes, she muttered, 'The hell with you Alexander Renaldo

Mendeneres.' She picked up the green wall phone and dialed. 'Helen, I can make it after all. You'll pick me up at three thirty? Fine, I'll be ready. By the way, what are we wearing? Terrific! I just bought a blue silk sari from Thailand. See you then.'

Forcing her mind to blankness, Dani switched on her stereo and allowed Roy Orbison to invade the small apartment. Dust cloth and broom in hand, she attacked the apartment with a vengeance. She then called the florist and ordered three dozen daisies with extra fern. To bake a chocolate cake or not to bake a chocolate cake? Why not? At two o'clock, she ran a hot tub and liberally laced it with exotic bath salts. Reaching for Stacy's latest western, she settled down in the silky wetness and started to read. If one were to attend a party given by one Stacy Whittier, then one had better know what his latest novel was about. Dani felt she could not, in all good conscience, drink his liquor and eat his food if she didn't at least have working knowledge of his latest creative effort. By the time she reached the end of chapter four, the hero had ridden into the sunset three times and had been dry-gulched twice. The bath water was also cold. She looked at the cover of the book and noted the price. Six dollars and ninety-five cents, and it was a very thin paperback. Ugh! Dani grimaced. Well, whatever turns you on, she grumbled as she stepped from the bath. Wrapping a cherry-colored robe around her slim body, she proceeded to make up her face.

Fifteen minutes later, she stood back to admire her reflection in the mirror. Definitely A-OK. Reaching for the atomizer, she lavishly sprayed Yves St Laurent and sniffed appreciatively. Holding her head at an angle, she twisted and twirled her long silken hair till she got the desired effect. Stepping into the shimmering blue sari, she had the feeling it had been made for her. Satisfied, she slipped into silver sandals. The soft cashmere shawl was the final complement to her attire. The doorbell pealed just as she cast a last look around the compact bathroom.

'Be with you in a minute,' she called. Dani checked the ashtrays, gave a last look around the gleaming apartment. Noting her reflection in the floor-length mirror in the small foyer, she winked at herself. The blue of the sari deepened her columbine, gray eyes. Heavy fringes of black lashes were shadowed against her high, prominent cheekbones. Her normally, wide, full generous mouth was pinched and drawn. Realizing that her emotions were altering her features, she willed herself to relax, shrugging her slim smooth shoulders to a more natural stance. Beneath the soft, rosy glow

75

of the lamp in the foyer, her dark hair gleamed with coppery highlights. Tucking a long stray strand behind her ear, she took a last appraising glance, this time grimacing at her reflection, and left for Stacy's party.

Valerie Mendeneres continued to flick the glossy pages of *Vogue* magazine, angry at the steady, insistent rapping on her apartment door. 'I'm coming,' she called indignantly. Smoothing the filmy gown over her hips and taking a critical look in the vestibule mirror, she moved to swing open the door. 'Eugene,' she said derisively, 'I told you I wanted to get some rest this afternoon! I'm simply exhausted by the trip and my head is aching!' Her slanted, turquoise eyes took in the form of Eugene's friend, Lou. 'And what's *he* doing here?' her voice shrilled. 'Look Eugene,' she added imperiously, 'I thought I told you I don't want any of your...' Her mind raced to find the word that described Eugene's friend.

'Oh pipe down, Val. Lou is a good friend of mine. You certainly are twitchy. What's with you? I live here, too, you know!'

'But let me remind you, Eugene, I pay the rent!'

'Nag, nag.'

'Don't give me that,' she spat. 'How do you think it would look to anyone who is anyone to see that ... that ... creep hanging

76

around here?'

'That's more like it, sis. I like it when you come down to earth. Those affected ways of yours get on my nerves.' Stepping closer to Valerie, Eugene placed an affectionate arm about her resisting shoulders. 'Ever since you married that "Cow King" of yours, you haven't been fit to live with.' His face broke into a slow smile that changed the normally hostile expression of his pale face to one of malice. 'I just brought Lou up for a drink. We've had a dry afternoon. Anyway, as I was saying...'

Lou reached for the glass that Eugene was holding out and plopped down on the arm of the sofa.

'Get your skinny ass off the sofa. You smell,' Valerie hissed, pulling the edge of her skirt away, dreading contact with the man's rough and seedy appearance. 'I don't want to have to pay any repair bills. Eugene is far too free with my money as it is.'

'I've been thinking, Val, about something you once said to me. You said it would kill Alex if anything ever happened to the kid. Knowing you as I do, I know that at times you can be incredibly stupid. You wouldn't be crazy enough to cut us out of this and make some kind of deal with your husband all by yourself now, would you? The kid for the scrolls, something like that, leaving you with all the money? I couldn't allow that,

Val,' he said threateningly. 'We're going to sell those scrolls. Together! If there's one thing we don't need right now, it's a kid.'

Valerie sputtered and cringed away from Eugene. She knew what he said was true and she hated him for being right.

'Where is she, Eugene?' she asked hesitantly.

'The last time I saw her, she was going into an apartment with some good-looking young girl. Let me start from the beginning. I knew what flight she was on, so Lou and I arranged to meet her. I didn't think we'd have any trouble picking her up, but I didn't count on the kid walking around as though she owned the place. That's what I thought when Alex didn't show up, that she'd be standing there crying her head off. Who the hell would have thought she'd go out and rent a limousine!'

Valerie smirked. 'And then, Eugene...'

'Well, she rode it to the UN and took the tour. Lou here has bad feet – I thought it was going to be too much for him.'

'Yes, I would think so...' Val said, wrinkling her nose, inching further away from Lou. 'And then...'

'Well, the whole time we were trying to get her alone, but the little ... but she was too smart. I had the feeling she knew we were there and what we were trying to do. Then she goes out into the park and picks up this young woman. After a while they took a cab to this woman's apartment and that's where she is now. We're going back to stake the place. You know, Val, keep an eye on things. I feel better knowing where she is.'

'Oh my, Eugene, how interesting! You've got a new plot for your next book! What is that drivel you write, is it science-fiction, westerns, what? I never can remember,' Val said with a sly grin, enjoying Eugene's discomfort at her allusion to his porn stories. Many a slur had been cast in his direction concerning his lack of expertise in writing anything above the level of smut. Eugene was driven by making a quick dollar and, his mind never far from the gutter, spun out reams of filth for five hundred dollars a pop.

'When we finish this deal, Val, and I have time to stop worrying how I'm going to feed myself, you'll change your mind.'

'Yes,' sneered Valerie, 'I suppose I'll have to.'

A chill washed over Valerie as Eugene closed the door. She didn't trust him an inch. There was an evil streak in Eugene and he would stop at nothing to gain his own ends. She knew Eugene would kill her without a moment's hesitation if he thought she was crossing him in any way. The turquoise eyes dilated with fear as she recalled her stepbrother's cold, merciless eyes.

A veil seemed to glaze Valerie's eyes as she

stared out of the wide, brightly draped window. If it wasn't for Maria, she probably wouldn't be sitting here now with this knot of fear in her stomach, spreading like some malignant cancer. This fear reminded her of the anguish she experienced the first time she had become convinced of her pregnancy and of the fact that she could no longer hide the obvious – even from herself.

How had it happened? A wild moment of passion, not love, never love. Whatever, it didn't matter now. What mattered was the fact that she had Alex over a barrel and he knew it. God! How she hated him! Hated him and that brat, Maria. There was no way he could beat her in this, of that she was certain. Long, miserable years at that stinking hacienda. He would pay for that and pay dearly!

Valerie laughed gleefully as she envisioned the look on his face when Maria didn't get off the plane. That's one up for Eugene, she chortled. Suddenly, she sobered. Still, if things got sticky, Alex would have to protect her. She was his wife and entitled to all the protection his name could give her.

Valerie closed herself in the master bedroom and flung herself down on the French divan which occupied one corner of the suite, decorated with a feminine touch.

Her mind buzzed, reeling backward in time and placing her once again in the garden outside the hacienda in Argentina. She had felt lightheaded then, so she had quietly stepped out to relax under the deep green trees to await the relief from her headache tablets. It was there, as she was lying comfortably and enjoying the winsome breezes, that she overheard the conversation between Alex and the *Senora*.

'I wish I could say something that would help you, Alex,' the *Senora* was saying, 'but I fear I cannot, my son. This is your responsibility and the decisions are yours. The secret was entrusted to you when you were but a child. Now that you are a man, I do not imagine it lays any less heavy on your shoulders.'

Alex had sighed wearily. 'Yes, *Madre*, I have been having the same nightmare lately: I've heard from Rome and they have instructed me to bring them the scrolls. And when I get to the cave, they are gone. The cask is open and I see that they are gone. I've no idea why I keep dreaming this, there is no one else besides you, *Madre*, who knows of the cave and its secret.'

'It is a shame that you could not entrust the secret to Valerie, as did the other Mendeneres men to their wives.'

'We both know why I am not able to tell her. Also, it doesn't seem as important since there is no son to pass the secret on to.'

'That is why, Alex,' the *Senora* said,

conviction in her voice, 'I am certain the secret will be revealed in your lifetime. With the world today, I have no doubt it will be soon.'

Afraid she would be caught eavesdropping, Valerie tiptoed quietly from her position in the garden. The tone that Alex had used was strange to her. And what cave was he talking about? There were no caves on the hacienda. She should know, she had ridden over every inch of the estate many times. And what were the 'scrolls'? Evidently something very valuable and very important to Alex.

Think, Val! She told herself. What kind of 'scrolls'? Scrolls were something old and anything old was valuable, worth money! Her eyes glittered at the thought. Worth money to whom? Cunningly, she wondered if they were something that could be sold to, say, a collector! Perhaps she could sell them to the highest bidder? That she didn't have the 'scrolls' somehow didn't matter. She would find them if it took the rest of her life. If they were valuable enough, they could set her up for life! I could leave this damn place and not have to beg Alex for a penny!

And what was that business about them being revealed in Alex's lifetime? Did they have religious overtones? Something like Bernadette and her vision? Within minutes, Valerie had changed into riding clothes and was waiting for her horse to be brought to her. She eyed the clean lines of the Morgan and felt pleased. He looked like he could use the exercise. Well, he'd get it today and tomorrow and every day till she found the scrolls. I'll call Eugene and see if he can investigate. And if I find them, he can put out some feelers for a buyer.

The stallion pawed and snorted as the young groom turned the reins over to Valerie. 'He's skittish today, *Senora*, but when he works off a little steam he'll give you a good ride.'

Valerie ignored the young Argentinian as though he had never spoken. 'Easy, Nero,' she said softly as she stroked the black satin head. She continued to croon softly as she mounted the animal. He reared back as Valerie held the reins. Gently, she loosened them and let Nero have his head. With a gentle nudge to his flanks, the Morgan galloped down the path. Valerie sat with ease and laughed as the scenery flashed by. It was the most exhilarating distraction at the hacienda.

For the remainder of the day she rode with her head down scrutinizing the ground. By the end of the day, she had found nothing. She returned to the farm in a fitful mood.

Time passed and Valerie followed the same pattern each day: she would dress, have the horse saddled, and ride out till nightfall. By the end of the second week, she hadn't discovered any opening resembling a cave. But Valerie, knowing Alex wouldn't lie, knew the cave had to be somewhere on the grounds. It was hidden and she meant to find it.

Angry and determined, she rode for another week and probably never would have found the clearing but for a crazy fluke of luck. The Morgan had shied at a rattle-snake on the path. Terrified, Valerie pulled on the reins and almost backed the horse into a huge gnarled tree behind her. Shaken from the experience, she dismounted and stretched her legs.

She walked on ever mindful of snakes, her eyes in the brush and ground. She bent down to pick a luscious flower and saw the darkness through the shrubbery. Slowly and carefully, she parted the lush greenery and saw the mouth of a cave.

It was so pitch black inside that she had to switch on the cigarette lighter that she had withdrawn from her jacket pocket. Instinct told her something valuable would not be near the mouth of the cave. Trembling with fear, she penetrated the darkness with the tiny flame of the lighter and walked deep into the darkness.

At best, it was a mere crevice in the rock formation but the farther she walked the deeper and blacker the cave became.

Finally she came to the end of the cave. A dead end and there was nowhere else to go. She cursed as she looked angrily around. This had to be the place, there wasn't another cave on the whole farm, she'd swear to it!

Valerie lowered the minuscule flame and dropped to her haunches. She pulled out a cigarette and lit it. The formidable boulder rocked as she sat down on it. Where the hell was it? Alex had said the scrolls, whatever the hell they were, could be found in a cask. Well, there wasn't any cask here!

Impatience over her near-victory made her angry. She jumped up and stumbled, the boulder tilted precariously, causing her to trip and fall. As she did so, the boulder tumbled over and Valerie lay with her mouth hanging open. She lowered the cigarette lighter's feeble flame and peered into what appeared to be a deep hole.

'Aha!' she exclaimed victoriously. 'Fortune does smile on those who persevere!' She laughed, the tinkling sound bouncing off the thick, damp walls and creating an echo that set her teeth on edge.

Carefully propping the small, square lighter against the rock, she reached down and withdrew a small cask. Holding it near the light she could see no way to open the top. It would have to be pried off. Valerie got down on her hands and knees, and, with the aid of the flickering light, she spotted a can of pitch and a sharp metal bar. She smirked to herself – it was almost too easy!

With clumsy fingers, she pried open the lid and withdrew an oiled, leather pouch. In this darkness, she wouldn't be able to see a thing. She cursed. Regardless of what was in the pouch, she was taking it. She plopped the lid back on to the cask and lowered it back into place. Struggling, she replaced the heavy rock and stood back to observe her handiwork. She ran from the cave, out into the sunlight, opened the saddlebag and jammed in the leather pouch.

With teeth chattering, she spurred the Morgan and galloped back to the hacienda. The biggest problem facing her now would be to get the pouch into the house without anyone noticing. Valerie rode her mount into the cool, dark stable and dismounted. She picked up a brilliant scarlet sweater that hung on a hook, and carefully placed it over the pouch.

Breathless, she made it unobserved to her room where she locked the door with shaking hands. Unraveling the strings of the pouch, she was all thumbs. Finally, after carefully unrolling one of the cylinders she held up an intricately written scroll headed with a multi-colored painting. 'Good Lord,' she exclaimed in awe. 'An illuminated drawing!'

'It's in Latin!' she grimaced to herself. 'Illuminated drawing! This is more stunning than any we studied in art class. They have to be worth thousands upon thousands of dollars.' If she remembered correctly, such things were only painted by monks.

Valerie opened the other scrolls. Each was the same as the first, save for the obvious difference in wording. Perplexed by their meaning, she carefully rolled each one back up and placed them in her tote bag.

Valerie waited until after the dinner hour to return to her room. There, she would call the airlines to inquire about flights to the States. She wanted to leave as soon as she could. She scribbled furiously.

Her eyes fell on the scarlet sweater she had used to hide the leather pouch. Her mind mused over how much money the scrolls would bring. She reminded herself to call Eugene. The way the flights ran in this God-forsaken country, it could be two days before she had a definite confirmation. The waiting time would give Eugene enough time to line up a deal. Anyway, she couldn't stay here. She couldn't take the chance of Alex discovering the scrolls missing. No, she'd pack and tell him that she had an immediate flight to New York. Then, if she did have to wait, she would stay at a hotel in Buenos Aires until a flight became available.

Impatiently, Valerie paced up and down in the confines of her room. She was nervous, which was to be expected, but a familiar strain of something else plagued her. Something she couldn't define. There were times when she had the eerie feeling that someone was watching her. She had experienced a similar sensation in the cave, but had shrugged it off. Could it be that damn monk they always used to talk about?

'Maybe it's my guilty conscience!' Hysterical peals of laughter filled the room at the thought.

Abruptly, her laughter ceased. Was that a sound she'd just heard outside her door? She tilted her head to listen. The tiny hairs on the back of her neck were standing on end. An icy chill seemed to penetrate her being. Quickly, she raked her eyes around the room. She sensed dark, sorrowful, ghostly eyes upon her. God! It couldn't be that crazy monk, could it? Holding her temples in a vise-like grip, she ran screaming – soundlessly – from the room.

Five

Dani woke perspiring profusely, her head pounding. God, what a hangover. That was some party! You really had to hand it to Stacy, he knew how to throw a party. Everything had been fine till everyone started to ask, 'Where's Jack?' From then on, she lost track of the gin and tonics. Come to think of it, she really didn't remember much of anything after that. She squinted at the clock: six thirty-five. She would have to get a move on or she would be late for work.

Holding her throbbing head to steady it, she swung her legs over the side of the bed. She shuffled her way into the bathroom and gulped down three aspirins, brushed her teeth and stepped under a needle-sharp spray of cold water. Shivering, she stepped from the shower and dried herself with a towel. She grabbed the first dress her hands touched, a mint-green knitted shift with a wide gold belt. Cautiously, she applied make-up and tottered into the kitchen to make instant coffee. She was just warming her hands around the bright, daisy-patterned mug when the phone rang.

'Oh, not this morning, not so early.' No one she knew ever called so early. Probably a wrong number, she grimaced, as she sipped the scalding coffee. The phone continued to shrill. Dani winced at the sound of the jangling phone. 'All right, all right. I'm coming,' she muttered. She picked up the receiver in the middle of a ring.

'Miss Arnold?'

'Yes?'

'This is Alexander Mendeneres. I feel that I owe you an apology.'

Dani waited as her head continued to throb.

'I wonder if I might stop by and speak to you, to offer my apologies in person. Also,' he added quickly, 'there is a matter I would like to discuss with you.'

'Look, Mr Mendeneres, I accept your apology, although I feel it is a little late coming. However, I happen to work for a living and right now I'm late for work. So give my regards to Maria – and goodbye,' she snapped in cold tones.

'Of all the nerve! Who does he think he is? Here I go out of my way to take care of this child and he accuses me of abduction, then he calls and apologizes and wants another favor. Not in this lifetime, Mr

Mendeneres. That's it, Dani Arnold, Sucker of the Year. Thanks but no thanks, Mr Alexander Renaldo Mendeneres,' Dani mumbled.

The subway ride was torture to Dani's throbbing head. By the time she reached her small office and saw the load of unopened manuscripts on her desk she felt the need for more aspirin. Her task accomplished and a cup of steaming coffee at her side, she opened the first manuscript – *Foxtrot to Death*. She shoved it back into its manila envelope. She opened another, *The Gelatinous Pawn*. This, too, went back into its manila envelope. Dani leaned back in her swivel chair.

Damn it, what does he want? Was something wrong with Maria? No, it was probably something ridiculous like the child wanting to come over to play with Bismarck. Speaking of cats, what was she doing with a cat? Young, single, and only a cat to love her. Talk about old maids set in their ways! Dani swallowed a hot mouthful of the coffee and tried to picture the lonely years ahead with the cat. Romance was out of her life for the moment. Who knows, at the age of twenty-six, I'm halfway over the hill. Still ... the deep, warm-toned timbre of his voice had affected her, charmed her with its inviting quality, ignited by a melodious Latin accent. She sighed, annoyed that she could be attracted, in any way, to one Alexander Renaldo Mendeneres. Pretty soon I'll have wrinkles, and Bismarck won't live forever. Gloomily, she envisaged a procession of Bismarcks in the coming years.

Dani swallowed the remainder of her coffee and once more reached for a manuscript. Ah ... *The ABC Affair*. It'll do for starters. Slowly, she started to read. Before she knew it, she was engrossed in the story. Lunchtime came and went. She turned over the last page of the manuscript and placed it back in its envelope to be passed on to one of the senior editors. It was good. With a little polish and some new terminology, it would be publishable. She glanced at her watch, ten past four. Not enough time left to get into anything new. She had a few hours coming to her and she might as well take them now. The headache was still with her, duller but still there. Going without lunch certainly hadn't helped. She gulped three more aspirins and called into her boss's office to tell him that she was leaving.

'Heavy date?'

Dani grinned. Let him think whatever he wanted – she didn't feel like explaining. 'See you in the morning,' she called.

The subway ride was mercifully short, and beating the rush hour was to her benefit.

Back in her gleaming, shiny apartment, she set about preparing her supper. Something light: poached eggs and some cream of mushroom soup. While the soup was warming, she poured some milk for Bismarck and cleaned his litter box. Washing her hands, she sat down to contemplate once again the phone call from Maria's father. 'Arrogant! I'll bet he's a real whiz with the ladies,' she snorted to Bismarck, who, in the process of licking his whiskers, managed to look like the cat that swallowed the canary. 'Do you know what I think, Bismarck? I think they should put all men on an island some place and blow it up. What do you think of that? Hmm. Well, maybe not all of them, but at least ninety-seven per cent of them.' At this declaration of percentages, the cat jumped into her lap purring contentedly.

'And that's another thing, Bismarck,' Dani muttered, dumping the cat unceremoniously on to the floor. 'There's no way that you and I are going to go through life alone. If I have to, I'll take a roommate.' As she removed the soup from the stove, the phone shrilled. Reaching with one hand for the phone, she carefully set the hot saucepan on to a trivet.

'Hello, Miss Arnold?'

It was *him*! One of the ninety-seven per cent. 'Speaking.'

'Miss Arnold. Please don't hang up on me. I must speak with you. It is very important.'

93

'I won't hang up on you, Mr Mendeneres. I am not that rude. Contrary to what you may believe, my parents taught me to respect my elders.' That should get him! 'What is it that's so important?' she demanded. 'And important to whom? I can't imagine what you have to say to the abductor of a small child that could be so important. Could it be that you wish to call the police?' she asked, her cold tone matching his of the day before.

'I do not blame you for being angry. I am most sorry. My daughter has explained everything to me. What can I do besides offering you my apologies?'

'I accepted your apology this morning. There is nothing further for us to discuss. I really must go now. My dinner is getting cold. Again, give my regards to Maria.' Quickly, she hung up the phone.

Sipping the soup she'd heated up, Dani swallowed each mouthful with one eye on the green telephone. Somehow she felt vaguely disappointed when it didn't ring. Her dinner over, she straightened up the bright kitchen, polishing the faucet to a bright shine. She changed into a faded pair of blue jeans and washed out the navy blue sweatshirt that proclaimed she was a student at MIT. A memento of some long forgotten boyfriend. As she bent to tie her sneakers, she decided she needed a drink.

She poured a considerable amount of gin and very little tonic, and gently squeezed the lime. Clutching her cigarettes and matches, she settled herself on the comfortable tangerine club chair. She propped up her feet on a matching ottoman. With the aid of the remote, she danced her way through the channels until she saw Dan Rather's comfortable countenance. She was paying rapt attention to the anchor's somber tones when the doorbell chimed.

'Come on in Martha, the door's open. Have a seat,' she said, not taking her eyes from the impressive-looking Rather.

'Miss Arnold?'

Dani jumped to her feet. It was the ninety-seven per cent again. 'I thought it was my friend, Martha,' Dani sputtered.

'Am I to understand, then, that if you knew it was me ringing your doorbell, you would not have answered?'

'You assume correctly,' Dani snapped. 'I thought we covered the apology on the phone?' Deliberately, Dani lit a cigarette from the stub of the previous cigarette. She took a long pull on her drink. Everything in moderation, she grimaced to herself. 'I would offer you a drink, but I know you must be in a hurry. So once again, give my regards to Maria.'

'Miss Arnold, hear me out. I don't blame you for being angry. I am trying to make amends. What more can I do? What can I say? Try to put yourself in my position. What would you have thought or done in the same situation?'

'For starters,' Dani snapped, looking him square in the eyes, 'I would have met my daughter at the airport. If that were not possible, I would have had someone do it for me. I can understand, though, that you were busy wining and dining a socialite and that was more important. I can read and my eyesight is excellent. The picture in the paper hardly did you justice, Mr Mendeneres. If that's your excuse, then you had better try again,' she said coldly.

'Miss Arnold, that picture was three days old. They must have put it in the paper as a fill-in. I was at the airport, the day of Maria's arrival. Somehow or other, she was on the wrong plane. Unfortunately, my mother did not see fit to inform me of the change in plans. My mother,' he said apologetically, 'thinks I can do all things – and reading minds is only one of them. Please believe me.'

Dani looked into the dark eyes and suddenly felt weak. God, he was a handsome brute. Suddenly, she found herself comparing him to Jack. This must be what they mean by separating the men from the boys. Feeling a giggle bubble in her throat, Dani said seriously, 'Very well, I accept your explanation.' Good lord, was that squeaky voice hers? What was he doing to her? She had never reacted like this to a man before. Hmm. No wonder that Alicia – whatever her name was – looked at him like some moonstruck calf.

'Papa, I cannot wait any longer,' Maria shouted from the open doorway. 'She did not hit you over the head. Can I come in now?'

Dani laughed and held her arms open and the young girl ran pell-mell into them, hugging her friend ecstatically.

'Oh, Dani, I have missed you. I told Papa how wonderful you are and how well you manage without the maid and the chauffeur. Is she not amazing, Papa?' the child asked beseechingly.

'I think you were absolutely right,' Alexander Mendeneres said seriously, a twinkle in his eyes.

'Did you see Bismarck? Is he not the most fantastic cat you ever saw? Dani says he is a tomcat and he goes on the prowl every couple of days. He has a girlfriend in the next empty lot.'

Dani suddenly choked on a mouthful of smoke.

'Any tomcat worth his salt has to have a girlfriend, wouldn't you agree, Miss Arnold?' Alexander Mendeneres asked, his eyes still twinkling.

'Oh absolutely, Mr Mendeneres,' Dani agreed. Both knew the statement for what it was.

'Is it time for *Batman* yet?' Maria asked. Dani glanced at her watch and nodded.

'Sit quietly, Maria. Miss Arnold and I have something to discuss. Perhaps we could talk in your beautiful kitchen? Maria has told me how lovely it is.'

'All right,' Dani agreed, leading the way to the small, compact kitchen. She was suddenly glad that she had cleaned it so thoroughly and that she had polished the faucet to a gleaming shine. Like he was really going to notice. She had to wonder if this elegant, handsome man had ever stepped foot inside a real kitchen. Alexander Mendeneres quietly closed the door behind him. Dani looked at it pointedly.

'Rest assured, Miss Arnold, you have nothing to fear from me. My attentions are most honorable,' he smiled.

Dani blew a stray wisp of hair from her cheek. So much for your intentions, but what about mine? She squelched the thought immediately. He was, after all, a stranger. What in the world was coming over her? She smiled, 'I just wondered what could be so important that you didn't want Maria to hear.' She looked into the mocking eyes and said quietly, 'You seem to have a poor opinion of me. Why is that?'

'On the contrary, I think most highly of you. That is why I am here. To put it simply, I need your help.'

'My help! How can I help you?'

'I would like to ask you to care for my daughter for a while.'

'What?' Dani shouted. That does it, she thought. The first dynamic man she had met in ages and all he wanted was for her to care for his daughter. God, why did he keep looking at her like that? His eyes made her want to help him but, at the same time, they irked her. What was it about this man?

'Naturally, I will pay you. My child seems to adore you. And,' he added hastily, 'she made a point of asking for you.'

'Now, wait just a minute. My responsibility ended with your daughter the minute you took her through that doorway. Besides, I have a job. I know hardly anything about children. Surely you can find someone more ... more adequate?'

Alexander Mendeneres looked at the tall girl. His eyes narrowed at her reluctance. He knew she would eventually come around. Why did she have to go through this rigmarole? Or would she? Could he be mistaken? Well he was a man and she was a woman, an attractive woman. He moved a step nearer and looked down into her soft eyes. 'Miss Arnold,' he pleaded huskily, 'I need your help desperately; and

Maria needs you.'

Dani looked into the dark eyes and felt as if she were drowning. She clenched her teeth. I'm behaving like a schoolkid who's got her eyes on the good-looking Math teacher.

She couldn't refuse. She knew that if she did, she would never see him again, and she did want to see him again. In fact, somehow it seemed like the most important thing in her life, to see this tall, dark, handsome, arrogant man again. 'I have a feeling we do things differently here in America than you do in Argentina. I have to think about it,' she said breathlessly, not wanting him to think she was too eager.

The dark eyes seemed satisfied, and yet the smile which touched his lips was absent from them.

'If I can arrange for you to take a leave of absence from your firm and pay you double the wage you receive now, would you consider it?'

'I don't understand any of this. Why me?'

'My daughter is my whole life and I want to be assured that she is well taken care of. I think you are the person to do this.'

Dani looked at the handsome man in front of her. Suddenly, he looked like a man at the end of his rope. His dark eyes held worry, tiny beads of perspiration formed above his upper lip.

'Why?' Dani asked bluntly. 'Just tell me why? And spare me the snow job in case you were contemplating one. In case you don't know what a snow—'

Alexander Mendeneres interrupted her. 'I'm fully aware of what a snow job is and no, I won't give you one. Now I see what my daughter means about your language. She said you speak divinely.' Suddenly he laughed. 'It is Maria's dearest wish to learn as much American slang as possible. You must teach her, Miss Arnold. This way she can teach her friend, Anna, on our return to Argentina. Now, as to why I wish this matter settled...' he said masterfully.

'My visit here in the United States concerns a religious article that has been in my family for centuries. It has been stolen. I have reason to believe that my wife, Valerie, is the culprit. She brought it into the United States, and it has come to my attention just recently that she has a buyer for this article. I only discovered a few days ago that a transaction was planned. That, by the way, is one of the reasons for my wining and dining, as you so quaintly put it. My wife hates me,' he said simply, his eyes reflecting his pain. 'She knows that I love our daughter more than anything on this earth, and she'll try to take Maria and threaten to harm her if I try to find the scrolls. But I must get them back – and I will have to use the child as bait to try and smoke Valerie out of her hiding place. And you, Miss Arnold, are needed to see that nothing happens to her. My wife is ... evil. I realize this must sound melodramatic to you. Believe me it isn't meant that way at all. If Valerie manages to get her hands on Maria, I can only promise you it will be the child's undoing. At times, I think my wife verges on the insane. Maria must never, I repeat, never be allowed to fall into Valerie's hands. I am trusting you to see that this never happens. At the same time, I must ask you to trust me.'

'You would use your own child as bait in this ... this affair?'

'I have no other choice, Miss Arnold. I must do this. Do you think for one minute that I enjoy it?'

Dani felt a wave of disgust and revulsion wash over her. 'How can you? What kind of father are you?' she asked in outrage. Alexander Mendeneres stood quietly, his gaze fixed on Dani's angry face.

'This sounds worse than any of the crazy, mixed-up plots that come across my desk every day,' Dani sputtered. 'If I say no, what happens to Maria?'

'I planned to ask Alicia Waverly to care for her. For some reason, Maria is violently opposed to the idea. She wants you. Will you do it, Miss Arnold?'

'I'm sorry Mr Mendeneres, but I don't

think I can help you.' Still put out by the curt treatment he had given her, Dani felt sore and wounded. 'I live a very different life from the one Maria is used to. I like your daughter, Mr Mendeneres – really I do – but I know next to nothing about caring for little children. Surely there must be someone else. I just don't feel qualified to take on the responsibility. I'm sorry. And another thing, I have worked very hard to get where I am now in my job – I can't just pick up without notice and leave. It's not fair to my boss.'

A muscle twitched in Alexander Mendeneres' cheek. He had to convince this strange girl to take on the care of his daughter. Suddenly, he knew that no one else would do. Now he knew why his daughter was so fond of her. For the most part, he had always found that he could trust Maria's judgement. Somehow he had to convince this tall, beautiful girl in the faded blue jeans that she needed him as much as he needed her. She was just what Maria needed. He would pay her anything she wanted. Still, the money hadn't impressed her. She must have some kind of weak spot. He simply had to find it.

'Do you read the papers, Miss Arnold?'

'Yes, of course,' Dani said puzzled.

'Then you must be aware of the upheaval and the religious struggle that is going on in my country?' At Dani's nod, he continued. 'The item my wife stole is priceless and a matter of salvation to my people. Simply put, it is a matter of faith.' The man looked at Dani with, what was it, hope, fear? Dani could put no name to the emotion that crossed the handsome face. She looked into his eyes and then looked deeper – there was no fanatic glitter in his eyes like the zealots she had seen on 42nd Street.

Still, she hesitated. Did she want to be burdened with a child to take charge of day and night? She wasn't really a swinging single, but she did have her moments. She would definitely be tied down. On the other hand, she needed a vacation and it would be a good chance for her to start her cookbook. He had said money was no object: she could take the child and go to Glen Garden for a few weeks, open the house and light the fieldstone fireplace and settle in for a while. She could see it now. She would be trying out new recipes in the large, homey kitchen. Maria would be in the living-room, in front of the roaring fire playing with Bismarck. Once more she looked at the tall, muscular man in front of her. She stared at him, making no commitment.

Alexander watched the doubt fade from the girl's face. He would give it one last chance.

'Very well, Miss Arnold. I can see that my

offer does not tempt you. I am truly sorry, for myself as well as Maria. I am afraid that I have taken up enough of your time.' He looked at the watch on his wrist and then into Dani's eyes. 'It is late. I'll have to take Maria to friends and, although they are busy people, I am certain that their maids will care for her. I have several contacts that I must make this evening. Thank you again,' he said wistfully. Dani almost groaned aloud at his tone. Men! He belonged to the ninety-seven per cent all right. The thought of Maria being tended to by an impersonal servant who, more than likely, would consider the child an inconvenience to say the least, flashed through Dani's mind.

'OK, OK, Mr Mendeneres. I'll do it. Let me be the first to tell you that wistfulness does not become you. Let's face it, you appealed to my basic instincts. You knew that I would keep Maria.'

Becoming businesslike, now that his daughter's welfare was provided for, he said, 'I don't know how long this arrangement will be. It could be a week, it could be as long as two months. Whatever, you will be well paid.' He reached into his inside jacket and withdrew a sheaf of bills and placed them on the table. 'This should cover any of your needs for the time being. I have already taken the liberty of seeing to your leave of absence. Everything was settled as of five p.m. this afternoon.'

'What?' Dani screeched, her face contorting in rage. 'How dare you interfere in my personal affairs! How dare you!'

'Miss Arnold, I told you I am a desperate man. I did what I thought was right and I have no time for recriminations now. You have agreed to the arrangements. One of my servants will arrive with Maria's luggage within the hour,' he said briskly, his tone a shade colder than his eyes.

'You mean it isn't out in the hall?' Dani asked snidely. 'Somehow I thought you came prepared for any and all things.'

The man smiled with his mouth transforming his face to someone quite likeable. At that split second, he fell into the three per cent bracket. Dani shivered as he extended his hand. At his touch, she felt a delicious tingle ripple down her spine until she looked into his frozen eyes. The delicious ripple coursed into a wave of abject fear.

She had never seen such eyes, but she could top that, she had never met such a man. How could one be attracted and fearful – all at the same time?

With trembling hands, she slid the bolt and slipped the chain into the brackets. A faint scent of the man's cologne seemed to hover near the door. She felt dizzy and light-headed. Was this man her destiny?

Six

When the ten o'clock news came on, Dani shooed Maria to the bathroom. 'Do a good job now, I want to see those teeth sparkle.'

'OK, Dani,' the child cried happily.

'I hope I did the right thing,' Dani muttered to herself. She really couldn't have allowed the child to be placed in the care of a maid, even though it would only be a temporary measure. Damn the man, he had conned her, pure and simple. There was no doubt in her mind that she had been conned by an expert. She cringed as she remembered the wistful tone. Well, it's too late now. She said she would do it and she never went back on her word. Plus she liked the child.

The child returned and grimaced, showing sparkling teeth. 'Did I do a good job?' she asked anxiously.

Dani smiled. 'Yep, let's see your nails and ears. OK, you check out A1. Now I showed you how to make up the bed, so hop to it.'

A week passed quickly with only one phone call from Alexander. Stash dropped by several times. Maria adored the bearded giant. Stash teased her unmercifully about growing up, so he could marry her. Maria was beside herself with happiness as he twirled her in the air at the same time, teaching her his favorite slang phrases. When the colossal man left the small apartment, it seemed too quiet and empty. She didn't know why, but she had a bad feeling that she was being lulled into a false sense of security. When the feeling threatened to engulf her, she would take Maria window-shopping and to various play-lands. They made many trips to the library – Dani to do research for her cookbook, Maria to raid the children's section. Maria made notes from the new American slang dictionary. They ate gourmet meals and both added a few pounds. The evenings were spent watching television and sending out for pizza, which Maria adored. Bismarck also took a liking to the stringy cheese.

The false sense of security disappeared when Nick from the pizza parlor delivered the fourth set of pizzas during the week. Dani shivered as she recalled his words: 'Miss Arnold, do you know those two men who keep hanging around outside the building?' When she had said no, Nick looked even more worried. 'They offered me five dollars to let them deliver the pizzas. One of them said he was an old boyfriend of yours, and it was a joke. They just don't look like your type, Miss Arnold – you got more class. Anyhow, I couldn't picture you getting together with some guy that wore a gold earring.'

Dani pretended to be puzzled and laughed it off. But she had told Nick that if it happened again, she would call the police.

Locking the door and settling Maria down with her pizza, Dani went into the bedroom and pulled aside the drapes. She looked down on to the bleak street and watched Nick cross over to the pizza van. As Nick pulled away from the curb, she saw two men emerge from a parked car. Cautiously, she stepped back holding the drapes in still fingers as she continued to watch. She trembled when she saw the two faceless forms glance toward her apartment windows. Were they the same two men that had been there the night of Maria's arrival, that day outside the church? Damn! She had meant to speak to the child's father but had forgotten. Watching a moment or two longer, she finally gave up her vigil when the men once again entered the waiting car. Dani knew that from where the car was parked they had a clear view of her apartment doorway.

Dani rejoined the child and sat nibbling cold pizza thoughtfully. She didn't recall if that same car had been parked in the same spot during the day. Tomorrow, she would have to pay attention. Should she call the police? And report what? That two men were sitting in a parked car outside her apartment? They would tell her that she read too many of the manuscripts that came across her desk. She shrugged and told herself that it was Maria's father's responsibility. Still, she had assumed care of the child, so it was now her problem. And, she added nastily, this cherished father had only seen fit to call once. Some adoring father, she snorted. As a substitute duenna, she was doing a heck of a lot better.

Three more days passed as Dani constantly watched from the window. The car appeared to change. By day it was a dark, maroon, beat-up Mustang. By night, it was a Chevy Nova, equally beat up. During the day, there was only one occupant in the car. In the evening, there were two. So far all they appeared to do was sit and watch the building. It was clear to Dani that they were waiting. She wished she knew what they were waiting for.

Dani and Maria left the church to strains of soft organ music. Amidst the throng of parishioners on the front steps, Maria grasped Dani's hand and pulled her toward the street. 'Hurry up Dani, hurry up. Can I run ahead for the Sunday papers and the jelly donuts? I'll be careful and I'll wait for you on the steps of the apartment.' Dani considered for a moment. She watched the busy street and saw nothing out of the ordinary. The two suspicious-looking men were nowhere to be seen.

'All right, honey.' Carefully, Dani counted out money and gave it to Maria. 'Stop in the deli and get me a box of rice and that's all. No goodies. You should get seventeen cents change, so you can get two pieces of bubble-gum. No more. And,' Dani said firmly, 'you don't chew it till after lunch.'

'Right on,' Maria giggled, skipping away.

There was a brisk chill in the air and Dani quickened her step. When she reached the deli, she peered through the plate glass. Maria was standing in line, patiently waiting her turn. Dani looked up and down the street. Seeing nothing to alarm her, she continued to her apartment. Still she was anxious. But surely nothing could happen to the child on a bright Sunday morning with throngs of people on the street, some going to the newsstand, others to the bakery.

What's for dinner? Perhaps a Spicy Shrimp Creole.

Dani de-veined the shrimp as she peered at the recipe with one eye. Her preparations completed, she poured herself a cup of fragrant coffee and sat down to type some notes.

The phone pealed and she reached for it with one hand, turning the computer switch to the off position with the other.

Bismarck emerged from the basket at the sound of the ringing phone. Stretching luxuriously, he looked around his domain haughtily and leaped with practised expertise on to the kitchen chair. He eyed the plump pink shrimp craftily and then turned to his mistress. The tabletop was forbidden territory as he had found, to his discomfort, on more than one occasion. Still, he studied the plump shrimp. To be quick as lightening was the key. With one leap, he was on the table scattering papers, getting one paw tangled in the electric cord and yet he was still inches from the bowl of shrimp.

'Aha! Caught you in the act! Off! Off! Wait till I catch you! Sixteen dollars a pound for shrimp! You'll get dried cat food for a week!' Dani screeched.

Bismarck's descent was only second to a streak of lightning. He was off the table and under the sofa in a split second. Dani grimaced, set the table to rights and made apologetic noises to Stash on the other end of the wire.

Seven

Eugene Whitcomb drove the dilapidated car around the corner and parked. 'Look,' he whispered, removing his sunglasses for a better look at the small figure bouncing along the sidewalk. 'It's her all right. She must be going to the deli. We'll grab her when she comes out.' Eugene scowled at the unexpected shadow that settled on Lou's face.

'I don't like it,' Lou muttered. 'Snatching kids is something else. Trouble, big trouble!' He continued to mutter to himself.

'Listen to me, we're not taking any old kid. This one is my niece. It's just like she'll be visiting us for awhile. We aren't going to hurt her. I have as much right to her as that woman who's watching her.'

'Yeah, that's right. That makes it different,' Eugene's skinny partner said, relief in his voice.

'We have to be careful,' cautioned Eugene. 'This kid isn't like other kids. God knows what she'll do when she realizes we're picking her up. Probably try to make a citizen's arrest,' he said sourly. 'Our best bet is to laugh a lot so, if she screams, people will think it's some kind of game. You know, Lou, you've seen how they do it in the movies.'

Lou nodded sagely. 'I like kids,' he said gruffly. 'You gotta promise not to hurt her.'

'Would I harm my own flesh and blood?' Eugene asked, a smirk slowly crossing his face.

'I dunno,' Lou scowled. 'I won't be a party to any rough stuff. Just remember that,' he said, hitching up his pants on his skinny frame.

'Here she comes. Get ready. Just pretend it's a game and we're the ones who have to win – the kid has to lose.'

Lou accepted this declaration with a smile. Eugene was right after all. She was only a kid. They were grown-ups.

Maria unwrapped her bubblegum as she skipped along. Punishment was a fleeting thing. Bubblegum was right now. 'One two, buckle my shoe, three, four, shut the door,' she laughed as she chomped on the chewy sweet. 'Five, six, pick up sticks, seven, eight, close the gate, nine, ten ... Hey—'

'Finish the rest,' Eugene smiled, as he grabbed one of Maria's arm and Lou reached for the other. 'We captured the fat hen!' Eugene laughed uproariously with Lou joining in.

Maria looked from face to face, puzzled. She didn't understand. 'Who are you?' She shouted to be heard above the shrill laughter. 'Let me alone! Remove your hands from me.' She looked at Eugene suspiciously. 'Are you molesting me?'

'Not on your life, kid. Would your own uncle molest you?'

'Uncle! You're not my uncle,' Maria screeched as she realized the men's intent. Eugene had the door open and was trying to force Maria into the car. Lou stopped dead in his tracks.

'You said you wuz her uncle. She said you ain't.'

Eugene gave Maria a violent shove and climbed in beside her. 'Don't open your mouth,' he hissed. 'If you do, I'll have to gag you. Come on, Lou, I said I was her uncle and I am. I can't help it if this kid's old man doesn't think I'm good enough for her. Would I lie to you?' he asked, watching the indecision on the tall, thin man's face. 'Get in the damn car before somebody comes along.'

'Yeah, I guess you're right,' Lou grinned. 'Rich people are like that. Figure we ain't good enough for them.' He eyed Maria silently as he got behind the wheel. 'He's a nice man, your uncle,' he said magnanimously.

'He is not my uncle,' Maria said between

115

clenched teeth. She looked at Eugene haughtily. 'It is a genetic impossibility,' she said, her voice ringing with authority.

'You should wash her mouth out with soap,' Lou said virtuously. 'Where did she learn them kind of words? You sure she's related to you?' he asked suspiciously.

'Yeah, yeah. Now shut up and drive. Take her to your place. Val will have a fit if I bring her to our suite.'

'You are kidnapping me! Don't try to deny it,' Maria yelled in outrage.

'You got it all wrong, kid. We're just borrowing you for awhile. Take it easy,' Lou coaxed.

'Do not tell me you are borrowing me. Only an idiot would believe that. You have the ulterior motive. What is it? I demand to know! Are you going to hold me for ransom? If so, I am afraid that on the open market I am worth very little.' She opened her hand. 'Seventeen cents and a box of Uncle Ben's long grain rice.'

Eugene shot her a disgusted look. 'Honey, your papa has a lot more than seventeen cents and a box of rice.'

Maria's mind raced. She had to think of something. Sister Theresa had said she would be the smartest one in the class if she would just apply herself to her studies. She knew she was being kidnapped. In the back of her mind, she knew it had to do with her

father and mother. Perhaps she could help.
I will get away, she thought confidently.
Besides I have the diplomatic immunity.
They would not dare to hurt me. Still, she
would have to act frightened.

Maria raised wide, frightened eyes to meet
Eugene's narrowed ones. 'I am afraid, sir,
that you are unaware of the mishaps that
have befallen our hacienda. We are almost
destitute. My papa is here in this city right
now, trying to borrow money just to keep us
alive. We are starving,' she added pitifully. 'I
am afraid he cannot pay for my release.'

'Jeez,' Lou said, 'how much does he need?
I got a little socked away, maybe I could
help him. I hate to think of someone going
hungry.'

'Lou,' Eugene yelled, 'shut up!'

Maria smirked to herself. 'The day I left,
there was but a crust of bread with a spoon-
ful of jam,' she said sadly. 'My poor old
grandmother wanted me to eat it. I could
not. I made myself think of other things. I
gave the crust to my grandmother and I ... I
licked the spoon,' she said dramatically.
'One has to sacrifice in these trying times.'

'You did that, kid?' Lou blubbered. 'That's
the nicest thing I ever heard of. Ain't that
the nicest thing you ever heard of, Eugene?'

'Shut up, Lou. She's pulling your leg and
you're too dumb to know it. Does she look
hungry to you?'

117

Maria tried to look hungry but it was hard with a mouth full of bubblegum. Still she tried. 'No, I am not hungry now. This kind lady took me and fed me and has offered me a home. I do not even know where my father is. He may be lying in a ditch somewhere ... starving.'

'Come off it kid, we don't have ditches in New York,' Eugene said nastily.

'She probably means an alley,' Lou said, stretching his neck to peer at Maria. 'Right kid?'

Maria nodded. 'And my grandmother, she may have starved by now.' Her words were pitiful. 'I am all alone with this box of rice and seventeen cents,' she said slyly.

Eugene, sensing his grand moment getting away from him, blustered, 'Listen to me you little twerp, stop playing on Lou's sympathy. He's dumb but I'm not. I know exactly what your old man is worth on the hoof, and that old grandmother of yours isn't wasting away either. So just shut up about it and stop trying to make Lou nervous.'

Maria hunched herself into a corner of the small car and sat silently, her eyes moving from Eugene, her uncle, to Lou in the front seat. Something had to be done. Dani would be worried. Would Dani tell her father? Of course she would.

What would Papa do? Maria wrinkled her nose and thought. He would say that if she found herself in a predicament she didn't like, then she would have to get herself out of it. She frowned, she wasn't sure if that theory held for kidnapping or not. Probably so, her papa was very firm. Rarely did he renege on a decision. She had to think. There must be some way for her to let Dani know she was all right. She cast a sidelong glance at Eugene. He was a little smarter than his friend in the front seat.

'Do you have a gun?' Maria asked anxiously.

'Why?' Eugene asked curtly.

'No reason, I just wondered,' was the nonchalant response.

'Well stop wondering. Park in the back, Lou – less chance of someone finding out what's going on.'

Lou swung the old Mustang around the corner and came to a halt. 'Home is where your heart is,' he chortled, as he looked at the dingy building.

Eugene dragged Maria by the arm and pushed her against the iron fence that blocked off a dirty-looking alley. 'Just stand still for a minute and don't move. No tricks. Understand?' Maria nodded.

Maria stood like a ramrod, and looked around. Depressing, she thought. She wondered what the conversation was about as she watched Lou and Eugene whispering near the fence. Whatever it was, Lou appeared to be upset. Eugene was gloating. Maria was puzzled. What did they want with her anyway? How did they know about her father? It must have something to do with the secret. She was sure of it. The secret and her mother. She watched as Eugene climbed back into the old car and drove away.

'Come on, kid, you come with me. I won't hurt you if you behave yourself.'

'I know that,' Maria said, her tone full of confidence. 'I could tell, just as soon as you started to speak, that you were the one with the brains. It shows,' she smiled.

'Really,' Lou smiled back.

'Oh my yes, that ... that man claims he is my uncle. He is not my uncle. I do not lie, sir.' She shook her head from side to side. 'I could tell right away, that you didn't believe a word of that. Why, anyone can look at him and see that there is not the faintest resemblance between us. I could see in your eyes that you didn't believe him, even when you said you did.'

'Yeah, you're right,' Lou said seriously. 'But he said he was your step-uncle.'

'That's not the same thing. That makes it artificial. Don't you agree?'

'Yeah,' Lou muttered as they walked up the dingy stairway. Wait till he got a hold of that Eugene. He was always lying to him. Artificial uncle! The kid had more smarts than Eugene would ever have.

Lou opened the grimy door and ushered Maria into an equally grimy room. 'It ain't much, but it's home,' Lou apologized.

'I find it ... quaint,' Maria smiled. 'It looks ... lived in,' she said as she noticed a run-down crooked rocking-chair. Everything was in one room: kitchen, bedroom, living-room.

'It's called an efficiency.'

'Yes, I see that, everything is very handy,' Maria smirked.

'Sit down, kid. Are you hungry? No? Well then, just sit here,' he said motioning to a chair. 'Eugene said I was to tie you up. Jeez, you're only a kid. If I don't tie you up, will you promise to behave and listen to me?' Maria nodded. She was glad he didn't say anything about not trying to get away. It was her duty to try and escape. She had seen a movie once and the prisoners refused to promise that they would not try to escape. It was something about the Geneva Convention. All they were required to give was name, rank, and serial number.

'Do you think I could have something to drink, Mr Lou?' Maria asked hesitantly.

'Sure, kid, but all we got is beer. You old enough to drink beer?'

Maria wrinkled her nose. 'Of course, do you think I'm a baby?'

'Well,' Lou shrugged, 'you never know. I don't drink it myself. Makes me dizzy.'

'Really,' Maria said, her eyes lighting up conspiratorially. 'Sometimes I get dizzy, too. Perhaps, later, we can get dizzy together.' She laughed at the joke and Lou smiled.

'You ain't so bad, kid. How come Eugene don't like you? He said you was different.'

'What do you suppose he meant? Do I look different to you?'

Lou shook his head.

'See, I told you, you're smarter than he is. How did you get into this kidnapping business? It could be dangerous. If I were some other kid, I would have screamed for the police and then where would you be? Crime doesn't pay,' she said virtuously. 'You should tell your friend that you prefer to make an honest living.'

'Yeah, you're right, I know. But see, it was like this. I work in a funeral parlor. It gets to you after awhile. You know, carrying and pushing those stiffs from one place to another.' He twitched his nose, and shrugged his shoulders. 'And that embalming fluid! Jeez! I can always go back if I want to. Most people aren't in a hurry to take those kinds of jobs. When Eugene asked me if I wanted to help and make some big money, I said OK. Not so much for the money, but just to do something different. He said it ain't exactly illegal, we would just skirt the edges.' Maria nodded understandingly. 'You know, kid, you ain't so bad. I thought you'd be screaming and carrying on like those wild kids on television,' he said happily.

'I know,' Maria smiled. 'That's what everyone tells me. Truthfully, Mr Lou, what good would it do me to carry on and cry and scream? I would only get upset and then you would get upset and then we would both be upset. So what is the point?'

'Yeah,' Lou muttered. 'What do you want to do? Do you want to listen to the radio or watch some television?'

'There is not anything good on Sunday morning and I have a headache, so the radio will bother me. Do you have anything to read?'

'Naw, you want something like *Peter Rabbit* or *Goldilocks*. I only have *Playboy*,' he said seriously. 'Let's just talk, I like to talk.'

'What do you want to talk about?' Maria asked conversationally.

Lou shrugged, 'Whatever you want.'

'Well,' Maria said hesitantly, 'who did you vote for in the presidential election?'

'I don't remember – Clinton, I think.'

'That was a poor choice. You should have voted for the one that said he would put chickens in every pot. Or is it two cars in every garage?' Lou looked blank.

'My father said your American presidents always make campaign promises like that. He said the two chickens always works.' Lou still looked blank.

123

'No one ever gave me two chickens,' Lou said belligerently. 'Guess I picked the wrong guy.' Maria couldn't help smirking.

'How do you feel about unions?'

'I belong to one,' Lou grinned. 'They ain't so bad the weeks they don't take out the union dues. What do you think?'

Maria laughed inwardly at the serious expression on Lou's face. 'I'm in favor of the four-day week. Actually, I can take them or leave them alone. I oppose abortion on the grounds that it is killing and I haven't made up my mind on acupuncture. How do you stand?'

'Jeez, them's all good things. I agree with you. You sure are smart.'

'I read a lot,' Maria offered by way of explanation. 'Mr Lou, could I ask you a favor?'

'What?' he asked suspiciously.

'You did say I wasn't kidnapped, didn't you?' At his nod, she continued. 'Well if I'm not kidnapped, could I make a phone call? Just to let the lady I stay with go buy her rice. She needed it for supper. She'll be waiting for it. That's not nice to make someone wait for you. Don't you agree?'

'Well, yeah,' Lou frowned. 'But somehow I don't think it's too good an idea. Eugene might get mad – in fact, I know he will.'

Maria, holding her hands in her lap, pinched the inside of her thigh, her eyes smarting with tears as she looked at Lou. 'I thought you might let me, Mr Lou,' she said tearfully.

Lou looked at the wet eyes and his heart melted. 'Well, if you promise not to tell Eugene. Just for a minute. Promise.'

'Oh, I promise.' She raced to the rickety table and was about to pick up the phone when it shrilled, making her jump. Lou also jumped. 'Must be Eugene, he's the only one who ever calls me. Him and the funeral parlor.' Hesitantly, he picked up the phone and listened.

'Lou, it's Eugene. How's the kid?'

'She's fine. Don't you trust me?'

'Did you tie her up?'

'Not yet, we wuz talking. She's OK, Eugene, she promised not to try and get away.'

'And you believe her,' Eugene demanded. 'Tie up that damn kid before I ring your stupid neck. You big jerk. Do I have to do all your thinking? At the rate you're going, we'll both end up in jail.'

'Why should I land in jail? I didn't do nothing.'

'In case you aren't aware of it, kidnapping is a federal offense.'

'You said we just borrowed her 'cause she's a relative. You better stop lying to me, Eugene. I don't like it no more.'

'For Christ's sake!' Eugene barked. 'It's

125

that kid, she's got to you. You stupid jerk. Tie her up right away and I'll be there in fifteen minutes.'

Lou lowered the receiver and narrowed his eyes. 'He called me "stupid jerk",' he said almost pitifully.

Maria quirked her mouth. 'What does he know? Don't listen to him. He probably voted for Clinton, too.'

Dani looked at the clock apprehensively. It was an hour since Maria had gone to the store. She should have been back by now. Perhaps she was talking to the doorman about the Yankees. She waited a few minutes longer and risked a glance out the bedroom window. The beat-up Mustang was gone. Her skin prickled in alarm as she picked up the phone and dialed the doorman in the downstairs lobby.

'Joe, this is Dani Arnold. Have you seen the little girl who's staying with me?'

'Not for a while. Not since the two of you left this morning.' Dani hung up and walked back to the kitchen. Perhaps she had stopped to play with Steve Myers on the first floor.

Not giving herself time to reconsider, Dani reached for a sweater and rode the elevator to the ground floor and literally raced for the deli on the corner.

'Mr Salerno, did you see the little girl

who's staying with me? I sent her for a box of rice.'

'Yes, Miss Arnold, some time ago, though. She said she had to go to the bakery when she left here. She bought a box of rice and two pieces of bubblegum. Seventeen cents in change. I was surprised she didn't spend the other two cents. Is something wrong?'

'She hasn't come back,' Dani said, a worried frown on her face.

'She probably met a friend of hers and stopped to play. Kids lose all track of time. I know, I have a few of my own. There's always one missing,' he offered kindly. Dani thanked him and jogged the short distance to her apartment. She rang the Myers' bell but there was no answer. A dog barked behind the door.

'Did she come back, Joe?' Dani asked the worried-looking doorman.

'No.' Anxiously, he scanned the almost deserted street. It did seem odd. The neighborhood had very few children and the little girl hadn't been around long enough to make any friends on the street.

Dejectedly, Dani rode the elevator to her floor. She couldn't have gotten lost. The child had gone with her many times to the market. It just wasn't like Maria to stay out this long. Should I call her father? What will he say? That I was lax in my duties and should have watched her more carefully?

She could almost see the anger suffuse his face. Justifiably so.

Back in the small kitchen, she poured herself a cup of coffee, her eyes on the shining wall phone. She alternated between the clock and the phone. Two hours had gone by and she had consumed six cups of coffee.

Where was the child? How could I have been stupid enough to let her go alone? What if some sex pervert had grabbed her? What if she had been kidnapped, by the men in the beat-up Mustang? Dani's stomach lurched at the horrible thought. What if some car had run over her and she had been taken to the hospital? She rejected the idea. Joe would have heard the siren and commented on it. He himself had looked worried.

Perhaps, though, her father had come by, seen her and picked her up. Perhaps there was nothing for her to worry about. That's it, she thought happily, he just picked her up and took her to the park or something. And not tell you? a niggling voice questioned. He didn't appear to be that kind of man. Even Maria had more sense, and she would have called by now.

Dani sat the mug down on the table with a thump and reached for the receiver. She dialed the number Alexander Mendeneres had given her and heaved a sigh of relief when he answered.

'This is Danielle Arnold, Mr Mendeneres,' she all but stammered. 'I don't know how to tell you this—.'

'Tell me what,' the cold voice interrupted abruptly.

'Maria is missing.' Dani forced herself to be calm. She told him what had happened and waited for his outburst. When it didn't come, she was shocked – almost speechless. In fact, he didn't seem worried at all. They must make fathers different in Argentina, she thought.

'What shall I do, Mr Mendeneres?'

'Wait. All you can do is wait, Miss Arnold. I am not blaming you.' His words were kind. 'I am sure that she is well. In fact, I can almost guarantee it. If you hear anything, please call me and let me know. And vice versa, of course.' The connection was broken abruptly. Dani sat on the yellow chair and looked at the receiver in her hand. Had she heard correctly? She shook her head to clear it. She went over in her mind the words the man had spoken. Again, she shook her head. She looked at the receiver as though it were a snake. Quickly, she replaced it and looked at her hands. She had to wash them. I must be nuts, she thought to herself. Or else he's nuts. Or we're both nuts. 'Well there's nothing wrong with me,' she said aloud, determined, 'so that leaves him.' Then why do you want to wash your hands? she asked herself anxiously.

'Just shut up, subconscious. I don't need any help from you today,' Dani muttered. She had to do something. What? She supposed she could clean the kitchen again, she could feed Bismarck.

These tasks completed, she made herself another cup of coffee. She sat with her hands clasped. The coffee grew cold and still she sat. The clock chimed five times when the phone shrilled. Dani looked at the innocent-looking box on the kitchen wall and hesitated. Slowly, she reached for the receiver and brought it to her ear, her heart thumping madly.

'Miss Arnold?' an oily, unctuous voice asked.

'Yes, speaking.'

The preliminaries over, the voice continued, 'I have something a friend of yours wants. Convey the message to him for me.'

'Are you speaking of Maria?' Dani asked. She knew he was, she just had to be sure and hear the words. She had to know the child was alive and well.

'You bet, sweetie,' the slick voice continued. 'Listen to me because I won't repeat it a second time. Tell Alex to call this number at exactly eight o'clock. The number is 555-8676. You got that? You could trace the number if you have a mind to, but then that big-mouth kid gets it in the neck.'

Dani waited, saying nothing.

'Right now the kid is OK. I only guarantee to keep her that way till eight o'clock. After that, her health depends on that old man of hers.' The voice was now virulent.

'I ... I'll try to reach Mr Mendeneres. Who shall I say called,' she asked inanely.

'He'll know,' the voice answered. 'Eight o'clock.' The line was dead. For the second time, Dani looked at the receiver. It seemed almost obscene. Wearily, she sat back on the iron chair. Her mind whirled and she felt dizzy. This couldn't be happening to her. She must be dreaming and this was one of the plots that came across her desk every day. She had carried it home with her and now she was dreaming about it. She gave herself a pinch on the fleshy part of her arm. Tears stung her eyes. She was awake, and this was no dream.

She carefully dialed the Mendeneres number and waited – five, six – 'Yes,' came the cautious answer.

'It's Danielle Arnold.' Quickly, she gave the message and waited.

'Thank you, Miss Arnold. I shall take care of the matter. You'll hear from me.' Once more the line gave off its pinging dial tone.

'Damn it,' Dani shouted to the empty kitchen. Bismarck, unused to such a sharp tone, scuttled under the table and looked at her with reproachful eyes. 'If he doesn't

131

care, why should I?'

Because this is all your fault. You're human, not to mention civilized, the niggling voice answered her. He's a robot. Robots have no feelings. I just have to wait. I have to occupy my mind. Keep busy, that's the answer.

Opening the refrigerator, she peered inside at the left-over food. Next, she removed the trash. She then cleaned the bathroom mirror. When she looked at the kitchen clock, she was dumbfounded to see that only fifteen minutes had gone by. Next, she called her office. No answer. Naturally, it was Sunday. What in the world had she been thinking of? She then tried Helen's number. The phone rang eight times before the answering machine clicked on. The lovely Helen was no doubt having brunch with the western writer, Stacy. 'I guess I can change the bed linen,' she muttered. Within minutes, the snug printed sheets were anchored firmly into place. Looking out the window, she noticed there still wasn't any Mustang. Sitting down on the flowered chair, she watched the minute hand of the small bedside clock make its tedious circle. Idly, she picked up a cigarette and laid it back down. I smoke too much anyway, she thought as she nibbled on her fingers instead, continuing to watch the small clock. The phone shrilled. Dani jumped off the chair.

'Hello,' she said cautiously, convinced it would be the oily, deadly voice.

'Dani, it's me – Maria.'

'Maria?' Dani exclaimed. 'Where are you? Are you all right?' What was the child babbling? Something about rice.

'Take down this number.'

'Maria,' she shouted, but the child continued.

'One minute. I only have one minute.' The phone was once more dead.

'I don't understand any of this,' Dani wailed. If she had been kidnapped, why was she calling on her own? And then all that talk about a box of rice. She sighed, looking at the number she had copied down. I must be losing my mind, she thought pitifully.

Dani lit a cigarette, all the while contemplating the number she had scrawled on the small note pad. Carefully, she dialed the number and waited. Seven, eight, nine, ten ... Suddenly, she slammed the phone back on the cradle. Her head reeled. Perhaps the child had managed to get to a phone and call when no one was watching her. Thank God she had hung up before someone answered and found out what the child had done.

She would have to call Maria's father and give him the number and let him handle it. She dialed his hotel and waited – thirteen, fourteen, fifteen. No answer. 'Oh hell,' she muttered, crushing out her cigarette in a crystal ashtray.

'Did I do all right, Mr Lou?'
'Yeah, kid, I guess so, but you shouldn't have given her my phone number. Eugene will have a fit. Come on now, I have to tie you up before he gets here.'
Maria looked properly crestfallen at this declaration. Her eyes were overly bright as the squat black phone shrilled.
'Don't answer that,' Lou warned.
Maria nodded.
'I hate to do this, kid. Honest.' Maria looked at him understandingly.
'I'll lay you here on the couch and you can watch some television.'
Maria lay quietly watching first one cartoon and then another. She didn't have the heart to tell Lou she preferred a more sophisticated program. Lou was laughing uproariously at the antics of the *Flintstones* when Eugene burst into the room. Seeing her bound and inert on the couch, he relaxed and smiled at Lou.
'I see the situation is under control. You had me scared for a minute, Lou. Come over here – I want to talk to you.' Lou untangled his lanky frame from the crooked rocking-chair and ambled over to where Eugene was standing.

'Yeah.'

'I got it all set up. I called the girl and she promised to have the kid's old man call me tonight. I gave her the number from the booth on the corner. Any tricks and the kid gets it.'

'Get's what?' Lou asked fearfully.

'Never mind.'

'How long are you going to keep her here, Eugene? I don't like it. She seems like a good kid. We had a lot of fun this afternoon.'

'I'll just bet you did,' Eugene said disgustedly. 'To answer your question, it all depends on her old man. If he comes across, then she can go tomorrow. If not, she stays.'

'You never did tell me what you want from him. You never told me anything about this caper except that I would make a lot of money and it wasn't exactly illegal. I don't like the whole thing. It smells.' Lou stuck out his jaw belligerently to make his point.

'What's with you? All of a sudden, this kid is getting to you. You weren't worried before. So what happened that you haven't told me? Come on, out with it.'

'I just don't like it,' Lou hedged. 'She's a nice little kid. I like her,' he added defensively.

'All right, so you like her. Great. She's a smart little brat, I'll give her that. You just let me handle this and keep your mouth shut.'

Eugene walked over to the bedraggled-looking couch and looked down at the child. 'Hey, kid, look at me!' Maria looked up into cold gray eyes.

'Yes,' she answered politely.

'I spoke to the woman who's been keeping you. She seemed worried about you.' Maria laid still and said nothing. 'I told her to have your old man call me this evening. You know your old man better than I do. Will he come through?'

'My father cannot be forced into anything,' Maria said quietly.

'What's that supposed to mean?' Eugene asked coldly.

'It means,' Maria said slowly and clearly, 'my father will pay you nothing for my release. He has principles.' The words were full of pride. 'Just about as many as your dear mama,' Eugene said snidely.

'My papa is not like my mama,' Maria shouted.

'Aha! I hit a nerve. That's some mother you have, kid. Even though she is my sister, she's a lulu. She'd sell you down the river for a lipstick. How come she hates you so much – her own kid?'

The harsh words stung Maria to the quick. She knew her mother hated her, but to have this repulsive stranger say it aloud made her want to cry. Her lower lip trembled as she lay mute.

'I thought that mothers were supposed to

tie ribbons in their daughters' hair and buy them pretty dresses, and take them to dancing school. What did you do that was so terrible to make her hate you? She won't even talk about it to me, her brother. And your old man, wow! She'd as soon stick a knife between his ribs as look at him. You sure come from a dizzy family. Come on, what did you do to her?'

Maria clenched her teeth fiercely to stop them from trembling. She gulped and answered calmly. 'It is a question of my birth. I was born a girl instead of a boy. All the Mendeneres' women have a son. It is important that the firstborn is a boy. As you can see, I am a girl.'

Eugene didn't know what he expected by way of an answer, but this wasn't it. He laughed cruelly. At the sound of the harsh laughter, two things happened simultaneously: Maria swung her legs from the day-bed and jabbed them into Eugene's midriff; the room darkened and a wind so strong and so fierce that the child gasped, swept through the room forcing Lou against the wall. Eugene brought up his hands to protect his face from the invisible force that was driving him against the wall next to Lou.

'It's the monk,' Maria screamed. 'It's the Mendeneres Monk and he's here to protect me,' she continued to scream making sure she could be heard over the careening sound of the wind in the room. Objects were flying about and crashing into the walls. Lou stood cowering in the corner as Eugene cursed loudly.

Suddenly, Eugene was moving across the room at a dangerous rate of speed. Maria, directly in his path, swerved to get out of his way. Eugene, his eyes dilated in fear, reached out to grasp Maria's arm to pull her to him. 'I don't know what the hell is going on but whatever it is, you better stop it and now, or I'll snap your neck,' he shouted. 'Now!'

'I told you, it's the Mendeneres Monk,' Maria laughed, enjoying the tumultuous chaos in the room. 'Do not hurt me. If you do, he will surely wreak his vengeance on you.'

'Whatever it is, call it off,' Eugene yelled as he brought up his free hand and slapped her on the side of the head. 'Call it off,' he screeched, his voice a high thin falsetto.

Maria blinked. 'Very well, but do not touch me again. Put me down. Immediately.'

'Brother Gian, it is Maria. I truly appreciate your intervention, but I think I can handle matters now. You see,' she said complacently, 'they do things differently here in the United States. I'm not sure anyone would understand our relationship.' She paused for a few moments and then continued impishly, 'However, I would appreciate it if you don't go too far away.'

Within minutes, the room was filled with sunlight and the air was once more quiet and still.

Lou was the first to recover. 'You should not have done that,' Lou yelled as he tried to twist Eugene's arm backward. Eugene, now nervous and confused, brought up his arm and knocked Lou to the ground with one blow. With a booted foot, Eugene kicked him in the ribs. Maria watched gleefully as the two men stood glaring at each other.

'Both of you listen to me,' Eugene yelled, hate emanating from his eyes. Maria looked at him through misty eyes. For the first time since entering the room, she was afraid. Afraid, not only for herself, but for Lou, too.

'I have to go see your mother, kid. When I get back I better not see any wind and Lou here smashed to pieces. You better be on that daybed just like you are now. Understand?'

Maria nodded. 'And you, Lou. Look at me!' Lou raised pain-filled eyes and stared at Eugene. 'If that kid isn't in the same position when I get back, I'll kill you. Do you understand? And no crazy wind and dark room will stop me. I've come too far to back down now. Oh, and kid, any funny tricks and that pretty lady gets it, too. Comprende?' Maria nodded again.

'OK. I'm going home to the apartment. I have some talking to do with your dear mama, about your dear papa. Then I have to come all the way back here to wait for your papa to call. After that, I'll be back here to check on you.' Eugene laughed shrilly as he slammed the door.

Silence washed over the dingy studio apartment, the television droning on in the background. Finally, Maria asked fearfully, 'Are you all right, Mr Lou?'

'I'm OK, kid. Did he hurt you?'

'I just have a sickness of the head. I'm all right. What are we going to do?'

Lou watched the child with fear in his eyes. He didn't know if he was afraid of her or Eugene. 'I have to think, kid. You lay here real quiet, so I can think.' For the moment he had a choice and he was going to stick with the kid. Maybe she was crazy, but then so was Eugene. She was different. She wasn't bad and she did call off that 'thing'.

Maria lay still and watched one cartoon after another. Lou waited for the end of the last cartoon before he untied her hands.

'Listen to me, kid. I ain't sure what I'm doing is right, I may be putting you in more danger this way, but I can't stand by and wait to see if that screwball is going to kill either one of us. I'm real sorry about all of this. I didn't know what he was planning. I guess I am stupid. I got a little money

140

stashed away. I just might take a trip somewhere after I take you home. You tell that lady that's watching you she better call the police and turn Eugene in. Do me a favor, though. Don't mention my name or where I live.' Maria nodded in agreement.

'Wuz you telling the truth when you said that your mom didn't love you because you wuzn't a boy?'

'Yes,' she said. At the sad look on Lou's face, Maria added, 'I do not mind now. In the beginning, it really bothered me. Now I am older and I understand better. She cannot help it. She is sick.'

'Jeez, imagine a mother hating her own kid. That's what made me decide. When you said that, and that jerk Eugene laughed, that was a dirty thing to do. You go wash your face and hands and comb your hair. I don't want no one to say I didn't take care of you. While you're doing that I have to get my stuff together.'

'Will you be all right, Mr Lou? He will not find you, will he?'

'Naw, I'll go underground. I got friends.'

Before they left, Lou turned out the lights and walked to the window and peered out. 'He's not there. Let me check the hallway first. I wouldn't put anything past that creep. OK, the coast is clear. Let's go.'

Halfway down the stairs, Maria stopped. 'I forgot the rice, Mr Lou. I cannot go home without it. Dani will think I am not dependable.' Quickly, she raced up the rickety stairs and was back in moments with the box of rice clutched in her hand. Lou smiled. She was a good kid, even if she could make wind and turn day into night. God, to think that crazy Eugene almost got his hands on her.

Eight

Alexander Renaldo Mendeneres arrived with the mailman. He looked at Dani coldly as he paced the living-room. 'You must leave here immediately,' he said curtly. 'I shall make the necessary arrangements. Be ready to leave tomorrow morning. I don't want a second attempt made on Maria's life.'

'Wha ... I can't possibly ... Just a minute...'

'You will do as I say. A motel perhaps. Preferably upstate somewhere. I'll decide this evening,' Mendeneres said briskly.

'I'm not going to any motel, here or up—'

'Miss Arnold, I will not repeat my directive again. You will leave in the morning.'

Dani flinched at the cold chiseled look on the man's face. 'Very well,' she capitulated. 'But,' she held up a warning hand, 'it will be to a place of my choosing and it won't be till Friday morning. Those are *my* directives. Take them or leave them,' Dani said frostily.

'Do you have a place in mind, Miss Arnold?' he asked benignly. 'Or are you exercising your women's lib authority on me?'

'If I were to do that, Mr Mendeneres, there wouldn't be much left of you even to discuss the matter,' Dani said icily. Quickly, she told him of her parents' home that was now hers and where it was located. 'So you see – it would be perfect. Maria would have other children to play with and then there's all that nice clean fresh air. But I cannot leave until Friday.'

'The house sounds perfect. Why didn't you tell me about it in the first place? Perhaps I was a trifle hasty in thinking you could be ready to leave by tomorrow. Friday will have to do,' Alex said abruptly.

'Why didn't I tell—?'

'The matter is ended. I will be in touch, Miss Arnold. You will guard my daughter with your life. Is that understood?'

'My life,' Dani said in a quaking voice.

Alexander Mendeneres' voice softened a degree. 'I don't think it will come to that, but if it does, yes, with your life. I hesitate to remind you of how well I'm paying you.'

'Don't let that bother you,' Dani said snidely. 'This isn't the first time you've reminded me of just how well I'm getting paid. Watch it, Mr Mendeneres, or you will be doing your own moving with your own child. There was never any mention of me parting with my life for your daughter. Your

144

money can't buy me. It would be wise if you remembered that little fact.'

Alexander Mendeneres moved a step nearer and the heady scent of his cologne washed over Dani. She blinked and backed away from him, a look of puzzlement on her face. He patted her shoulder gently. 'I had no idea, Miss Arnold, that you were so emotional. Enough,' he thundered. 'You will do as I say. No more and no less. I will be in touch.' Once more, he patted her shoulder in a paternal way.

'Yes, sir,' Dani found herself saying – quite meekly.

Once Maria had been returned and Dani felt the little girl hadn't been traumatised, she made the decision to leave the small apartment. She picked up the phone and dialed. 'Mrs Alpert, this is Dani Arnold. I'm fine and you? Good. I'm planning on coming up to the house for a while. I wonder if you could arrange for the utilities to be turned on. Could you have one of the kids take off the dust covers and air out the house? I plan to leave Friday morning.' She listened for a moment. 'That's just fine, Mrs Alpert. You still have the key, don't you? I certainly do appreciate it. By the way, I have a little girl staying with me.'

Dani laughed. 'She's ten. I think Kelly will like her. She's ... different.' Dani hung up smiling to herself.

'Listen, sweetness, it's time to clean the litter box, so hop to it. I have another call to make.' Dani dialed. It was picked up on the first ring.

'Stash, Dani.'

'Hi, how's it hanging?'

'Can't complain. Stash, I need a favor, no questions asked. I need some wheels for a while. I'm sorry but I can't be more definite than that.'

'No sweat, I can let you have my jeep with four-wheel drive or my VW Beetle. You name it.'

'I'll take the jeep. Are you sure you don't need it?'

'You know better than to ask. What are friends for? When you're done with it, just park it behind the coffeehouse. You want the jeep delivered?'

'I would appreciate it. Could you arrange it for Friday morning?'

'Eight o'clock suit you?'

'Perfect. Thanks, Stash. Oh, one other thing. If it isn't too much trouble, could you check my apartment from time to time?'

Stash chuckled. 'Lovely lady, your wish is my command. Take care, Dani. If for any reason you need me, just whistle.'

'Thanks, Stash,' Dani said softly.

Back in the kitchen, she inspected Maria's handiwork. The litter box hadn't been cleaned, just new litter on the top. There was cat food on the floor and some dribbling down the counter.

'Maria?'

'Yes, Dani?' the child asked.

Dani remained silent and just pointed to the litter box and spilled cat food.

Maria grimaced. 'You do it, Dani. My papa pays you to take care of me – I don't have to do that. Besides,' she said petulantly, 'it's a messy job, and I'm tired.'

'Sit down, young lady. I think you and I better get something straight right now.' Forcefully, Dani maneuvered the belligerent child to the wrought-iron chair. 'First of all, I am not your servant. You will do what I tell you and there will be no complaints. Is that understood?'

The child twitched on her chair with downcast eyes.

'Bismarck is my pet and I have taken care of him for a good many years. I can continue to do so. I don't need you to help me. I did, however, think that you liked Bismarck and would want to help with his care. I see I was mistaken. When it is time for me to give you your dinner I will spill half of it on the floor and the other half on the counter. Whatever I don't spill, you may have. And,' Dani said sternly, 'there will be no pizza.'

The child raised miserable eyes to meet

Dani's. 'I am sorry.'

'You probably are, but that doesn't change anything. You will not play with Bismarck today or tomorrow. You are not to take him into bed with you. Is that understood?'

The child nodded.

'I'm not finished yet, Maria. Now you can clean up the mess you made and re-do the litter box.'

'OK, Dani. I forgot, right?'

'You better believe it.'

'Right on,' the child said happily as she set about cleaning the litter box. 'What's for dinner tonight?' she asked.

'Shrimp Creole, if I ever get it made. But don't be surprised if it tastes like cat food,' Dani said picking up a moist lump of jellied meat that had landed on a plump shrimp.

Maria giggled as she worked. Dani smiled at the easy affability of the child.

Dinner over and the small kitchen cleaned, Dani suggested they make popcorn. Munching contentedly in the colorful kitchen, she tried unsuccessfully to reach Maria's father. Finally, she gave up in disgust. The popcorn bowl empty, she peered through the slatted blind, the Chevy Nova was nowhere in sight. She looked for the Mustang, but it wasn't in sight either. 'Thank God,' Dani said softly.

The doorbell pealed and Maria raced to the door. 'Who is it?' she called. 'It's Papa,' she squealed, unlatching the door.

Dani looked at the tall man with reserve, her pulse quickening at his cool glance. She felt confused. Maria was shooed into the bathroom for her shower while Dani opened the discussion heatedly.

'I tried to reach you for over three hours to let you know Maria was safe and unharmed. You weren't there,' she blurted childishly. Alexander Mendeneres offered no explanation. 'I thought you would want to know,' she said as her heart pounded. Quickly and concisely she repeated the child's story and waited for his reaction.

'It was my wife's brother, stepbrother actually,' he explained. 'There is nothing to worry about now. He'll not have the nerve to try again.'

Alex's voice conveyed the exact amount of confidence he wished to impart to her. But the man's voice on the phone telling her that he had Maria was still all too fresh in her ears, still ringing with menace and chilling her blood with all its implications. 'Well, Mr Mendeneres, if you won't worry I guess I'll have to display my woman's intuition and worry for the both of us,' Dani shot at the unruffled Alex, feeling the unmistakable effect of his voice upon her.

'I got a look at those two characters on Sunday afternoon after church and they looked pretty unsavory to me! And don't try to chalk it up to my feminine hysterics!'

A smile broke out on Alex's sun-bronzed face, beginning with his eyes, making them glint with amusement and then spreading to his mouth. 'Querido...' he murmured, disguising a bubble of laughter ... 'I see you've gotten yourself into a ... what is the word?'

'Snit, Papa!' Maria offered.

A bolt of lightning shot from Dani's eyes, piercing both father and daughter. She seethed inwardly, glancing from man to child, noting the similarity of expressions on their faces. Why does he have this effect on me, Dani wondered. I've never followed anyone so blindly. Why did I have to start now? She met Alex's eyes unabashedly, flushing slightly as she recalled the term of endearment – usually reserved for Maria – with which he had just used to address her.

'I know you think me callous and uncaring, Miss Arnold. I'm not. You will just have to take me on faith and accept me as I am. There are things you do not understand. I knew the child was safe. I could have laid my hands on her within a matter of minutes after you called me. My stepbrother has not been out of my sight for days. The matter is ended, let us say no more,' he said arrogantly.

'What kind of father are you?' Dani almost shouted. Why hadn't he told her he'd known Maria's whereabouts? Why hadn't he told her before? Or brought Maria back sooner? She felt confused and weary. Why does this have to be happening to me? And this man, why did he attract her so? One minute she wanted to melt and fall in his arms, the next she wanted to spit and claw at him like some cat. And that tongue of hers, it must be forked. Was it because she had to assert her independence? Did she want him to see that she was her own person? She knew deep within her that she would agree with any-thing he asked of her. Oh, she would argue and fight but she would give in. It must be that old devil sex. Well, if that was the name of the game, she would play even if the rules were drawn up by Alexander Mendeneres. She couldn't help herself.

'Why can't you tell me what's going on? How do you expect me to care for your daughter without knowing? I refuse to be kept in the dark. I'm sorry I agreed to this whole thing. There is something fishy about you, Mr Mendeneres. In fact, I'll go one step further and say you're downright smelly.' Seeing the beginning of a smile at the corner of his mouth only incensed Dani.

'My dear, Miss Arnold, I've never in my life come across a female as exasperating as you,' he said throwing his hands in the air. 'How many times must I tell you that I know exactly what I'm doing? For the last time, I am using the child to draw Valerie

151

out into the open. Nothing will happen to the child with you guarding her. I have every confidence in your ability, and my own,' he said conceitedly.

'What if something goes wrong? I don't have eyes in the back of my head. Any number of unforeseen things could go wrong.'

'There is no other way. The scrolls must come first; even before Maria. Nothing will go wrong. As long as you are in my employ, you will do as I say. I have no intention of telling you that again. If I feel there is something for you to know, I will tell you. Comprende, Miss Arnold,' Alexander said imperiously.

'Yes, sir,' Dani said meekly.

'The matter is settled. Liberated women, spare me.' His tone was insolent.

'Are you trying to say that women belong in the home under their men's thumbs?' Dani asked sweetly.

'Precisely,' came the urbane reply.

'I agree,' Dani said in a syrupy voice. 'Women belong in the home and that is where they should go directly after work.'

'Enough,' roared the voice.

'Chauvinist,' Dani muttered through clenched teeth. 'Very well, Mr Mendeneres. Since we are to leave here, I'll draw up a rough map and give you directions to my country house. As soon as I have the phone

152

connected, I'll call and give you the number.'

'Very well, I shall call every evening at ten thirty. Will that be satisfactory?' Dani nodded. With one hand on the doorknob, Alexander Mendeneres turned, 'As to the kind of father I am, let us just say I am not ordinary. I love my daughter very much and am concerned with the world that she grows up in.' Suddenly, without any warning, Dani felt soft, warm lips on her own. She hadn't known a kiss could speak of such tenderness, such yearning. She felt herself lifted, transported to a place of strength and security. She felt a response from somewhere deep within her stir and ebb to the surface. Her lips clung to his in answer to his demand. She pressed closer, willing him to enfold her within his strong arms. Dani surrendered to the moment, wrapping her arms about him, pressing herself to his body, feeling his hard muscular vitality. Slowly, he gripped her shoulders causing her to wince with pain, as he extricated and disentangled himself from her embrace.

She looked into cool, mocking eyes, his mouth set in a tight grim line.

The moment left her stunned. Disbelief and indignation at his rejection knotted in her throat, as she tasted the bitterness of gall.

'So you are not quite so tough as you

pretended, Danielle Arnold from Brooklyn. I thought not,' he said mockingly as he twitched her chin.

Dani gasped. He actually twitched her chin, just the way a father does to a child. 'Don't kiss me again,' Dani said, trying to regain her dignity.

Cool, mocking eyes narrowed and his cutting remark brought her back to reality. 'You shall be more careful how you speak to me in the future.'

Dani suffered under the sting of his verbal thrust. 'That is, if I ever speak to you again.'

His eyes warmed with humor and he quietly stated, 'You shall, Miss Arnold, you shall.' He turned then and self-assuredly strode out the door.

Dani slammed the door and kicked it viciously, as warm salty tears coursed down her cheeks.

Alexander Mendeneres, outside, heard the violent kick that Dani gave to the heavy paneled wood. Beyond the apartment door, he shed his pose of self-assurance and somberly strode toward the elevator. 'If you only knew, Querido, of the torment that stalks my soul, hunts me into the recesses of my conscience. Can I barter my flesh and blood – more – that which is part of me, the light of my life, my reason for existence? And for what? Mere pieces of parchment upon which some monk wrote the words of an angel.' Even as the thoughts raced through his mind, he knew he would. He would have to and his only assurance that Maria would remain safe was his belief and faith in the mercy of God.

Alex stepped out of the apartment building and walked slowly to his car across the deserted street. The blackness of the night cloaked him like a shroud, befitting his depression. Across the narrow street he glanced back at the building which housed his precious little girl. He lifted his eyes to the halo of light emanating from Dani's window. Bright, cheery. A home, he thought. How long since that word 'home' had meant anything other than hostile, repressed feelings and haunted, empty rooms.

Nine

Since money was no object, Dani headed straight for Saks and Bergdorf Goodman. By three o'clock, she felt as though they had bought out the children's department.

Maria's antiquated pleated skirts and Peter Pan collars were replaced with blue jeans, sweatshirts, shorts and T-shirts, along with sneakers in every color of the rainbow. A multi-colored windbreaker and yellow slicker completed their purchases.

'Let's go home, honey. By the time we get there, the packages will start to arrive. Both stores have promised delivery by six o'clock. I want to stop at the drugstore and the library to get some books for you to take with us.'

Dani again woke to rain. She hurried from the warm bed to pull aside the draperies. The dilapidated Chevy was in its usual place. Dani glanced at her watch: seven fifteen. Wracked with fear, she ran to the phone and dialed. 'Stash? Dani. Did I wake you?'

'No,' came the sleepy deception.

'Would you do me a favor when you leave the car?' Quickly Dani explained about the Chevy Nova. Stash asked no other questions.

'I'll take care if it, Dani. Don't worry about it. You want I should keep anyone on the apartment? No problem. Take care, Dani. Remember, we have a date for the Super Bowl game.'

'I won't forget. Thanks again, Stash. And Stash?'

'Yes, Dani?' Poor Stash, his voice always sounded so hopeful.

'Stash. Feel free to drop around the house anytime. We'd love to have a man around to cook for.'

'Gotcha, Dani! You can make book on it. I'll be seeing you real soon.'

Dani dropped the receiver into place. 'Good old Stash. I can always count on him. No questions asked. With men like him around, I have to go and fall for a nerd like Jack. Eeeech!' She shuddered in self-disgust.

Dani showered quicky and dressed. She was scrambling eggs when Maria walked sleepily into the kitchen. 'Oh boy, am I hungry.' She peered into the frying pan and licked her lips. 'Is it OK if I pick up Bismarck now, Dani? The two days are up.'

Dani smiled. 'All right, but hurry and get

157

dressed. Don't forget we leave today, rain or no rain.'

Dani placed the crisp strips of bacon on a paper towel, put bread into the toaster and scooped out the fluffy, scrambled eggs on to warm plates. She poured frosty glasses of orange juice and then fixed herself a cup of coffee.

Dani carried her cup to the bedroom and opened the draperies. The car was gone. There was no sign of activity below. There was also no jeep. Perhaps Stash had parked it in the back or around the corner. It wasn't like Stash not to come through. Where was Stash?

Breakfast over, the apartment cleaned up – all the appliances turned off, ashtrays cleaned and emptied, luggage by the door, Dani glanced at her watch. It was nine fifty.

'Are you ready, Maria? Do you have all of Bismarck's toys and his catnip?'

'Yes, Dani,' the child answered, holding out a large wicker basket that was to be Bismarck's home till they arrived at the little house called Red Top, in Glen Garden.

Dani took a last look around the tiny apartment. Quickly, before she could change her mind, she ushered the child through the door and locked it up. Once in the small lobby, she looked at the mountain of luggage that, for the most part, represented Maria's new wardrobe.

'Ready, Miss Arnold? Your friend left the car around the corner. I waited for a free parking space and then I moved it for you. It's right outside. Here are the keys,' the doorman said as he bent down to pick up the luggage.

'Fine, Joe. Come, Maria.' Dani walked through the door and immediately bumped into Maria. Bismarck howled his outrage at this rough treatment.

'Oh!' squealed Maria. 'Is it to be the parade? Is your president to be here? Oh!' she squealed again. Dani could only gasp. She looked around to see if there was another jeep on the street. She found there wasn't. This was it. She shielded her eyes as Joe came up to her with the luggage, a smirk on his face. 'It certainly is different,' he grinned.

Dani continued to gasp and Maria to squeal. 'No, the president is not coming and no there is no parade,' Dani said sharply. 'We are the owners of this ... this ... magnificent ... vehicle.'

'You are making the joke? You mean we truly get to ride in this ... this car?' Maria asked happily.

Dani squinted at the jeep. It was painted an overall luminous chartreuse. There were hand-painted, luminous peace signs and vines of all shapes and sizes. In between, there were red, white and blue stars.

159

'Definitely nauseous,' Dani gulped. Well, once inside she wouldn't have to look at the horrendous monstrosity.

Maria, beside herself in glee, was busy touching first one painted star and then another. 'And they don't rub off,' she gurgled happily.

'I didn't think I could be so lucky,' Dani grimaced. She stowed Maria in the seat beside her, gently placing Bismarck's basket in the back seat. She saluted Joe and put the jeep in gear. They were off with a flourish. Dani looked in the rear-view mirror and saw Joe grinning from ear to ear.

The trip was uneventful, although they did cause quite a commotion when they swung on to Route 31. Dani headed south and straight for River Road. Once in the hills, no one paid the slightest bit of attention to the two girls and the brilliant jeep. Dani watched the now familiar terrain and almost missed the turn-off for Hollow Road. Quickly, she flashed her signal and skidded around the corner. 'We're almost there, honey. Just up the road a bit.'

Maria looked at the heavily wooded road and exclaimed over the brilliant colors of the leaves.

'Here it is,' Dani said, pulling into the driveway, a catch in her throat. It was home. It would always be home. Suddenly she felt safer than she had in days.

She looked first at the eighty-foot tulip tree that stood in the middle of her front yard. She had expected to see a mountain of leaves. Kelly must have raked the yard for her. He was a good kid. In the summer, he mowed the grass and in the fall he raked the leaves. When she had tried to send him money, he had returned it. Soon he would be making his confirmation and she could repay him with a gift.

'How do you like it, Maria?'

'Oh, Dani. It is truly beautiful. Where is the brook? Where is Kelly? Where are the ducks? Where is everything?' she babbled happily.

'First, let's do things one at a time. You take Bismarck into the house and let him out of the basket. I'll carry in the luggage. By that time Kelly will be over here and he can show you everything else.'

'Will he like me, Dani? What kind of name is Kelly? I don't know any saints named Kelly.'

'Kelly is a nickname the kids gave him. It's short for Kelher and of course he'll like you. You are the most beautiful kid I've ever seen. He'll love those long curls. Hurry up before Bismarck takes a fit.'

'Does he have a girlfriend here, too?'

'Nope. He has about two dozen girl-friends. Each time I come up here all the owners of lady cats lock up their pets.'

Dani traced her fingers lovingly over the warm, cherry tabletops that were graced with brass lamps. She choked back a lump in her throat as her fingers touched her father's pipe stand. An overwhelming feeling of nostalgia engulfed her. Far back in the ignored recesses of her memory, she could hear her mother's voice calling to her father telling him tea was on. Her nostrils sniffed at a whiff of remembered hush puppies dripping creamery butter. Everything was the same. Her mother's treasured collection of Waterford crystal, the big, deep, old-fashioned sofa that one could lose oneself in, her father's books, the feeling of warmth and love. Everything ... the same. Her glance fell to the fireplace and the brass firedogs. There it was, the chip on the edge of the firedog and her mother's voice, 'But Jim, they were such a bargain and they remind me so much of the pair my grand-mother had.'

Dani looked around the familiar room. Matching love seats in an apple-green pattern and a light flanked the massive natural fieldstone fireplace, which was the focal point of the whole room. A high-backed wing chair covered in deep tones of russet brought a smile to her lips. She could almost see her father sitting there lost in his book. The perimeter of the floor was shiny oak. Nestled between the love seats was one of her mother's prize possessions, an imported oriental carpet in shades of oyster white, soft Nile green and buttercup yellow. The effect was one of overall tranquility.

Dani basked in the remembered conspiratorial wink her father had shared with her whenever anyone mentioned another of the flea market bargains.

Everything was cleaned and fresh smelling. Mrs Alpert must have cleaned the house, her and her eleven kids. Dani walked into the kitchen and opened the refrigerator. Hmm. Milk, juice, eggs, bacon, fruit and bread and butter. At least they wouldn't starve. 'Let's unpack and then you can get acquainted with the neighbors.' An hour later, the girls were settled in and there was a rap at the door. Maria raised hopeful eyes.

Dani grinned at the child who stood mute in her new blue jeans and striped pullover, navy blue sneakers and blue bows in her long curls. She looked good enough to eat.

'Come in,' Dani called.

The screen door opened hesitantly and a redheaded boy with a freckled face peeped in. 'Hi, Miss Arnold,' he grinned.

'Come on in, Kelly. I want you to meet a friend of mine. Maria Mendeneres, this is Kelly Alpert.'

Kelly stuck out his freckled hand. 'Hi,' he grinned.

Maria gave him a small curtsey and

chirped out a greeting.

Dani groaned. 'Ah, Kelly, she needs a little help. See what you can do, will you?'

Kelly grinned. 'I can see that, Miss Arnold. I'll do my best,' he said looking at Maria doubtfully. 'Come on, twerp, let's go,' he said to the suddenly bashful Maria.

'Does he mean me?' Maria whispered.

'You're the only twerp around. So I guess he does,' Dani grinned.

'Terrific,' Maria grinned in return as she followed the freckle-faced Kelly through the door.

'Mozel tov, Miss Arnold.'

'Same to you, Kelly,' Dani laughed. 'I can see it's going to prove to be an interesting vacation.' Funny, Kelly made no comment on the garish jeep. Probably sees them every day, Dani thought.

The days of early October turned into weeks for Dani and Maria. Kelly and his friends had the entire month off. The grammar school had burned to the ground in the late spring and the new school wouldn't be ready till the middle of November. Dani found her days to be busy and was making remarkable progress with the cookbook. She'd even sent the first four chapters to her boss and received a glowing letter of praise. The evenings were spent quietly watching television or going to a local movie.

Maria spent her time with Kelly and his

164

small band of friends. She was up at dawn and would fall asleep by nine o'clock from sheer exhaustion. Kelly had been as good as his word. He watched over Maria like a mother hen. He put up with her feminine ways and was slowly turning her into a tomboy ... Dani winced when she thought of how Alexander would react to the new Maria. But the child was deliriously happy. She trotted after Kelly like a puppy and he only had to speak and she was his slave. Kelly, however, did not take advantage of the child. Maria became as adept at 'kick the can' as Tony Russo, and could shimmy up a tree better than Danny Ryan. Kelly praised her to the hilt when she became better at knot-tying than he was. The only lull in the child's day was when the boys were occupied with paper routes or their confirmation classes.

Dani was busy making chocolate chip cookies for the children to take on a picnic when Maria asked, 'Will he invite me to go, do you think, Dani?'

'Invite you where?' Dani asked, as she carefully measured sugar into a big earthen-ware bowl.

'You know, his confirmation.'

'I don't know, Maria. Has he said any-thing? The Alperts usually have a party for something like that.'

'He has not invited me, and I want to go.

Tony and Danny are to go. They said so. Maybe because I am a girl they won't want me there.'

'I don't think being a girl has anything to do with it. I'm sure that you'll be invited. If you are, you will have to start thinking of some gift to give Kelly.'

'I have already thought of that, Dani. When my father calls tonight, I will ask him what gift I should give. Will that be all right? I wish Kelly to have the plane ticket to come to Argentina for the Christmas holiday. Kelly said there is no school here for the Christmas season. Do you think that would be a good gift?'

Dani considered. 'Has Kelly made any mention of wanting to visit Argentina?'

Maria nodded. 'He said he would like to visit someday when he is rich. I know, if my father buys the ticket for Kelly he can get them for Tony and Danny and they can come together. Wouldn't that be the greatest?'

'Absolutely,' Dani grinned. She had no doubt that Alexander Mendeneres would agree to the plan, regardless of the cost. If Maria wanted it and it was within his power, he would do it.

'What are you doing in the house anyway? Where are Tony and Danny?'

'Tony had to go to the dentist and Danny is delivering his papers because they came early. Were you here when the school burned down, Dani?'

'No, but the children will have to remain in school an extra month next summer, did you know that?'

'Sure. But the boys said they would rather be off now. It is lucky for me that they have no school, right?'

'Absolutely.'

'Hey, Maria!' A shout came from outside.

'They are back. So long, Dani. See you later.' She was gone before Dani could blink.

Dani resumed her baking and kept one eye on the clock. Promptly at five, she removed the last tray of cookies from the oven and slid in a tray of veal lasagna. She turned down the oven to low and sat back to enjoy a cup of coffee. She was munching on a piping hot cookie, with her feet propped on the corner of the table when she raised startled eyes to see a form standing in the doorway.

'I knocked, but there was no answer,' Alexander Mendeneres said, picking up a cookie. 'Delicious,' he said.

'I didn't expect you, Mr Mendeneres.'

'Can't we dispense with the formalities? Call me Alex.'

Dani nodded. She did not, however, tell him to call her 'Dani'.

'Where is Maria?'

'Maria is out with her friends. She'll be home in time for dinner which is at six o'clock. Would you care to join us?'

Alexander nodded. 'I would be delighted.'

'Would you care for a drink?' At his nod she raised questioning eyebrows.

'Scotch, if you have it.'

Dani nodded and prepared the drink and made herself a gin and tonic.

They carried the drinks into the living-room and sat facing each other on the love seats that flanked the fireplace.

'How is Maria? Has there been any more trouble?'

'Maria is fine. There has been no more trouble. I do feel that I better warn you that there has been a change in Maria. I am not too sure if you will like it. I, however, approve of it heartily.'

'Then I will bow to your judgement,' Alexander agreed gallantly.

'Ah ... I hope you feel that way later on,' Dani gurgled.

'I take it she has conquered the American slang.'

'Oh my, yes. Maria is definitely a pro now. Like she says, she can really "flip the bird". I'm not sure what that means myself but I haven't the nerve to tell her I don't know. And how is your project going?'

'I have made excellent progress. My goal is in sight. That is why I came here this evening. I think in a few short weeks, the matter will be closed. I wanted you to know that so you could make your own plans.'

Suddenly, Dani felt lightheaded. The child would be leaving. She had grown so fond of her. And this strange man that made her pulses quicken when he was near. It was all about to come to an end.

'I'm glad that you were so successful on your ... I wonder, though, if I might ask a favor of you? I promised Maria to have a Halloween party and to take her trick or treating.'

'I think that can be arranged.'

They made small talk. Dani, for some reason, getting more uncomfortable by the minute. Alexander Mendeneres looked at the large, square watch on his wrist. 'It is six fifteen and the child is not here.'

'Don't be alarmed. Kelly is usually very prompt. I am sure they got involved in some game and they will be here in a few minutes. In fact, I hear them now.' Dani turned her head to the wild giggling and laughter coming up the driveway.

'Miss Arnold is going to skin you alive, Maria.' It was Kelly speaking.

'Oh no,' Dani groaned. The door suddenly opened. Dani closed her eyes at the sight that met them. There stood three shame-faced boys with a wild-looking caricature of the pretty child that had left her kitchen an hour before. She was muddy from head to toe, green slime dripping off her. One plump toe wiggled from a hole in mud-caked sneakers. Clutched in her fist was a fat, green garter snake. But that wasn't the worst. Dani looked at the child's head. Where in God's name was her hair?

'Miss Arnold,' Kelly quavered nervously. 'We sort of had an accident.'

'It was my fault, Dani,' Maria shouted happily. 'The boys told me not to jump in the pond, but Danny said only boys with long legs could do it. I could not let him rip me off – right, Dani?'

'Absolutely,' Dani giggled, still looking for the long curls.

'Well, when she fell in the pond she got all that long hair tangled in the weeds and it looked like it was going to pull her under, so we cut it off with my pocket knife,' Kelly blurted.

'Wha ... you cut my—'

'Be quiet, Alexander,' Dani said sharply, 'I will handle this.'

'Now I look like the boys. Only,' Maria said sadly, 'their hair is longer than mine. I am so happy,' the child squealed, 'and look, I have the snake. They said I couldn't catch it. Where can I keep it?' Suddenly the child seemed to take notice of her father for the first time. 'Hiya, Pop,' she shouted as she squished into the kitchen for a box.

'Hiya, Pop!' Alexander Mendeneres barked.

'I thought I told you to be quiet,' Dani
snapped. 'When I want you to speak, I'll tell
you.'

'Good work, boys,' Dani said. 'I'm proud
of you, and many thanks. How about some
cookies?'

The boys nodded.

'Ah ... Miss Arnold, you won't punish
Maria, will you?'

'Of course not. Let me introduce you to
Maria's father.'

Three small boys stood at attention for the
introduction. All three manfully stuck out
their hands to be shaken. All muttered
polite phrases while Dani giggled on the
sidelines at the expression on the man's
face.

Maria carried in a plateful of cookies and
handed them to the boys.

Danny chose a cookie and sniffed. 'Gee,
Maria, you smell.'

'Yeah,' sniffed Tony. 'You'll have to soak in
Mr Clean. That's what my mother does to
me.'

'Great,' Maria gurgled happily. 'What's Mr
Clean?' she whispered to Dani. 'Do you
have any?'

Dani nodded. 'It's under the bathroom
sink. Get a move on and make sure you
clean up the bathroom. If you leave a mess,

you'll redo it tomorrow.'

'Right on, Dani. I'll do a good job. Here, Pop, watch my snake for me,' she said, putting a shoebox in her father's lap. Alexander Mendeneres sat, his mouth hanging open.

'You look better with your mouth closed, Alexander,' Dani grinned.

'Did ... did ... you see my daughter?' he exploded.

'Of course. But I also saw a deliriously happy child. Tell me, have you ever seen your daughter so happy?'

'No ... but...'

'No, but what?'

Suddenly the man laughed, actually roared. 'She called me "Pop" and did you see her hair?'

Dani joined his laughter. 'She certainly was a sight. Wait till you smell her after her bath.' They both convulsed in laughter.

Crushing out her cigarette in an onyx ashtray, Dani watched the man opposite her. The transformation when he laughed was amazing. He looked like one of the ads in the Sunday paper that depicted the aristocratic country gentleman. He certainly was a handsome brute. Remembering the feel of his lips on her own, Dani felt her pulse start to throb. Carefully schooling her face to betray nothing, she looked into the dark eyes opposite her and flushed.

172

Somehow she felt the man was thinking the same thing she was. Go careful, Dani, she admonished herself. You can get hurt too easily. He's from a different world, a world that you don't belong to. He could never be seriously interested in anyone as plebian as herself. Still, in unobserved moments one could let one's imagination run rampant. Again, Dani remembered the feel of those lips on hers and wished she had the remembered feel of those strong arms to complete the picture.

'I think I better see about dinner,' Dani said quietly. 'Would you care for another drink? No? Well, then if you'll excuse me...' Dani walked into the huge kitchen and removed the bubbling tray from the oven. Opening the refrigerator in her muddled state, she swung the huge door too fast, causing it to slam against Alexander who had followed her into the kitchen. Dani leaned over to grab the door and lost her balance. Alexander caught her and held her for a moment. Neither moved for a space of a second. Suddenly his arms tightened and Dani's picture was completed. She closed her eyes, there seemed to be no will left in her body. She waited for the expected kiss. Opening her eyes and gazing into warm, brown laughing eyes, she was momentarily taken off guard by the laughter in Alex's eyes.

The arms tightened perceptibly. 'I never break my word, Miss Arnold,' the man said, mocking.

Dani sputtered, disengaging herself. She felt shaken and humiliated. Damn the man.

'Set the table,' Dani said through clenched teeth. 'Your daughter will be out here in a moment.'

Alexander began to set the table with meticulous care. 'I have never had to do this in order to be served a meal,' he said, smiling with his eyes into Dani's furious face.

'Things are tough all over, Mr Mendeneres. If you're not careful, you'll be doing the dishes when you're finished.'

'Oh,' he drawled the word. 'And if I do what will be my reward?' he teased.

Dani was about to offer a squelching reply when Maria entered the kitchen. Clean blue jeans and sparkling white T-shirt and hair standing on end. She looked like a porcupine. Dani, unable to contain herself, giggled, as did Maria. Not, so far, her father. He looked in outrage at his daughter.

'I'll tar and feather the young whelp,' he roared.

'Oh, Pop, cut it out,' Maria giggled. 'Dani can fix my hair. She can do anything,' she said magnanimously.

'She can, can she?' Alexander roared.

Dani stood back and reveled in the man's discomfort. This was her moment and she intended to savor it.

'Kelly's father doesn't get upset over things like this,' the child muttered. 'Neither does Danny's father, and Tony's father says it is all part of growing up. I adore their fathers, and they like me. They said when I leave here, I will be as American as apple pie and hot dogs. You are outdated, Papa,' Maria said defiantly.

'Outdated?' Alexander roared. 'Outdated, am I?'

'Yes,' Maria said in a shaking voice. 'Is it not so, Dani? He does not act like the other fathers.'

Dani made a very obvious square with her two hands. 'Very definitely,' she said seriously, watching the fury and the indignation show across the aristocratic countenance. 'However, Maria, I did tell you that when you return to Argentina you would have to revert to your old ways. This is a case of when in Rome, do as the Romans do. Your father, unfortunately, does not do things the way most Americans do. And,' she said viciously, 'that covers other things as well.' Dani saw by the flush in the man's face that she had scored. She went one step further. 'Most American men,' she said, her eyes on Alexander Mendeneres, 'are not quite so mockingly gallant.'

Alexander Mendeneres looked at the irate girl and said softly, 'Touché, Miss Arnold.

The next time I will not keep my word like the gentleman I am.'

Dani flushed a rosy pink and started to toss the salad.

'Dani, can I be excused from dinner? I want to go punk picking with the boys. I can take a peanut butter and jelly sandwich with me.'

Suddenly, there was a clatter on the back porch. Three faces peered through the screen door. 'Can you go?' Kelly yelled.

'Can I, Dani?'

Dani pondered the question. If she gave the child permission, she would be alone with Alex. If the child stayed, it would definitely be a strain to force herself to be polite for her sake. 'Yes, you can go. Did you boys eat?'

'No,' Kelly answered, 'but my mother said she will make us some hot dogs when we come back.'

'All right. Maria can go,' Dani said.

'Ah ... Miss Arnold ... can Maria smoke the punks?'

'Sure. What's the sense of going punk picking unless she can smoke them?' Dani answered as she saw the fury mount in Alexander's eyes.

'Remember, Kelly. Home before eight and watch out for her.'

'OK, Miss Arnold. Come on, squirt. Let's go.' Maria marched out the door happily.

176

Dani heard the boys compliment her on her new hairdo. Kelly said she looked like a skinned rat. Tony proclaimed that she looked better than his dog, Duke. Danny said now she wouldn't have to comb her hair for weeks. Maria, in her element, thanked them profusely. Alexander Mendeneres looked as though he were on the verge of an epileptic fit.

'Could I get you an Alka Seltzer, Mr Mendeneres?' Dani asked sweetly.

'Did you hear how they spoke to my daughter?' he choked. And, 'What is this that you say she can smoke? I won't have it. Do you hear me?' he said pounding his fist on the table.

'Really? What won't you have? First of all, since you don't have the faintest idea of what smoking a punk entails, why are you interfering? Do you think I would let the child smoke? All they do is light the tip of the punk and it smokes. I grew up around here, Mr Mendeneres, and that is one of the kids' greatest pastimes. As for the boys' compliments on your daughter's hair, they were only being honest. She does look like a skinny rat. She does look better than Tony's dog and true, if need be, the child won't have to comb her hair for a week. Now tell me what is so terrible? Well, I'm waiting, Mr Mendeneres. Don't tell me that the cat has got your tongue. Usually you are quite articulate.'

Dani set the tray on the table with a loud thump. She walked over to the salad, but she was suddenly pinned again in those familiar, strong arms. Gently, she was turned till she faced him. Dani raised cold, defiant eyes to meet the burning Latin ones of the man who held her. She felt tears smart her eyes as she continued to gaze into the dark pupils of the man. The arms tightened and she felt warm lips once more on her own. Suddenly, with the strength of his arms around her, she felt wanted, desired. Dani returned his kiss with every fiber of her body, answering in a language of its own, a language of love. For Dani now knew the meaning of that elusive emotion and she reveled in her new-found know-ledge. Time was meaningless. Finally he broke away, much to Dani's regret. He held her at arm's length and smiled.

'Forgive me, I had no right to kiss you. I am a married man. For a moment, I forgot.' The dark eyes were racked with pain. 'If things were different, perhaps ... Your lovely dinner is already cold.' Once more his eyes took on the aloof quality that Dani had noticed before. Following his lead, she sat down on the chair he held out for her. Dinner was a quiet affair. They left the dishes on the table and retired to the living-room to await Maria. Dani fixed drinks and they sat opposite each other on the love seats flanking the fireplace. Dani felt cold, and shivered involuntarily. Alexander noticed the chill and quickly offered to light the fire.

'Hi, everybody,' Maria cried happily. 'Boy, am I pooped. I have to go to bed early. Kelly is taking me fishing at six thirty. Goodnight, Dani, goodnight Pop,' she said, grabbing him in a bear hug and kissing him soundly.

'See ya,' she yawned.

Dani smiled at the child's retreating back and moved her eyes to the man lighting the fire and knew that he was all she could ever want in life. Him and the child that she had grown to love. Even that would be ripped away from her when it was time for them to leave. Feeling like part of her body was slowly dying, she chided herself – no self-pity. There was always Bismarck.

Her eyes bright with tears, she spoke to the man.

'You must tell me of Argentina.'

Dani watched Alex's broad back as he bent toward the hearth to light the kindling. He sat effortlessly on the floor, one arm draped over his knee as he seemingly concentrated on the glowing embers, as little by little the kindling sparks jumped and ignited the waiting logs until they burst into a dazzling, dancing fire.

Like me, Dani thought, waiting for his

179

touch, so I can feel alive. Her glance strayed to the broad, yet graceful hand on his knee, and the desire to feel that hand in her hair and touching her neck welled within her.

Sensing the draw of her emotions, Alex turned and Dani felt a hot flash as his eyes swept over her. She held her breath as he came and sat beside her and silently took her into the folds of his embrace. Wordlessly, they understood, and each savored the close moment for what it was, each knowing the futility. Dani raised her eyes to his, catching a sob in her throat as she felt the impact of the sadness of his eyes. Her self-pitying thoughts were blown away and in their place came a resolute longing to ease his pain, to cradle his head against her breasts.

With a low moan, his lips came crashing down upon hers and she invited their warm pressure. When he drew away from her, she felt a vast loss and he saw this in her eyes.

'Querida,' he whispered softly, 'come closer to the fire where you'll be warm.' He motioned her to a place on the rug before the now blazing fire and sat down a little distance from her where, she knew, he would not be tempted to take her into his arms.

'Remember I told you of a family relic which Valerie brought here to the States?' Dani noticed his upper lip curl almost indiscernibly – each time he mentioned his wife's name. Inwardly, she felt a small triumph. 'Do you?' he asked.

'Yes, Alex, I remember.'

'This religious article is not your usual sort, where superstition is the embodiment of its value. Listen carefully, Querida; the story I am telling you is long and intricate, and it is important to me that you understand.'

Listening to his deep, resonant voice, Dani found herself incredulous at the implications his tale wove for her.

'For five hundred years, my family has been guardian to the "Future Scrolls", and now the duty has fallen to me.' His face displayed the seriousness with which he considered his duty. 'The secret has always been passed on to the oldest son when he reaches the age of fifteen. On the birth of the first son, the secret is entrusted to the child's mother so that in the event something unforeseen should happen to the heir, the secret will not die with him.

'My mother raised me with a belief in duty and a responsibility to the scrolls. When I came to college in the States, I was so enamored with Valerie's beauty I was blind to her perfidious shallowness. Her whole life has been a sham and in a great way I've been much to blame. She had not the character with which I, at first, credited her.

Life in Argentina was dull, with none of the excitement and color which Valerie demands.

'Maria's grandmother saw through Valerie at once and was greatly troubled, although to her credit she never by word or deed made her sentiments evident to me. In all truth, I don't believe I would have listened.

'When Maria was born I was confused. You see, Cara, the first born to the heir of the secret has always been a son. I suppose I made much of having a son before Maria was born and Valerie, sensing my confusion when I was told the child was a girl, mistook it for disappointment. Her frustration was multiplied when she was told she would never have another child.'

Dani saw his eyes cloud and noticed the cleft in his chin darken and appear deeper. She knew what agony it must be for a man of Alex's reticence to tell her these things.

'I was disappointed at first, but I always loved Maria. Who could help doing so?' His face brightened. 'From the first, she was a remarkable child, precocious and endearing. Later, much later, when discussing this with my mother, she said that when Maria was born it was her belief that the secret of the scrolls would come to light during my lifetime, hence the break in the male lineage. It seems, Querida, Maria's grandmother was correct in her assumptions.

Waiting for me in Argentina is a letter from the Pope. I feel I can safely assume that the time has arrived when the burden will be lifted from my shoulders.'

'Alex, if the mother is only told on the birth of a son, how did Valerie come to learn of the scrolls?'

The corners of Alex's handsome mouth turned downwards. 'Among Valerie's adroit attributes, eavesdropping is very high on the list. From what I can gather, Valerie overheard a conversation between my mother and myself. By this time, she had built up an overwhelming animosity toward me, an animosity which spilled over on to Maria. Discovering the shared secret between my mother and myself enraged her. She felt left out, discriminated against. Like a snake shedding its skin, Valerie changed, her hatred of me surfaced and I later discovered how long she plotted to learn the whereabouts of the scrolls. I truly believe, Querida, she did not steal them with the intent of a pecuniary gain, it was revenge against me, the Mendeneres heritage, and her own incapacity to be a part of it. It was her step-brother who, when she told him of her discovery, enticed her to bring them to New York and peddle them as an objet d'art to the highest bidder, as though they were a souvenir from a tawdry carnival.'

'Alex, how could she have gotten the

scrolls through customs?'

'That is where the secret was to her gain. No one would suspect that some writing in church Latin would be of any value. Besides, Valerie was equipped with the story that the scrolls were a gift from our family to a church here in the States.'

'If the scrolls are as unimpressive as you say, Alex, could Valerie sell them, too? The secret has been so well guarded, surely she could not convince someone to pay an enormous sum of money for a relic that hasn't been authenticated!'

'You surprise me, Dani, you are very quick. I neglected to tell you that the scrolls contain illuminated drawings. Brother Gian was an artist of great talent. Even Valerie could recognize the beauty of the illuminations with which he began the principal part of each scroll.'

'Alex, are you saying you've read the scrolls? You've actually seen them and studied them?'

'Never! They are in old church Latin and the artistry is intricate. They would take a great deal of time to study. I am saying my father showed me the scrolls when I was fifteen and pointed out the magnificent illuminations which they bear. Immediately afterward, he replaced them in their pitch-lined urn and re-sealed it with wax, the exact manner in which the first Mendeneres brought them to Argentina.

'I hope you understand why I must do everything in my power to regain possession of the scrolls. As I mentioned, there is a letter from Rome awaiting me in Argentina. My country is more in need than ever before of the renewed faith which the scrolls can instill in my people. They are suppressed religiously by the political regime and many have lost their fervor and faith.'

'That fact is true almost everywhere, Alex, not only in your country. I believe that's the reason today's youth are seeking these new religions and practicing them fanatically. They're searching, Alex, to find something to fill the emptiness within themselves.'

'Yes, Querida, and perhaps the Holy Father sees this the way you do. Dani, the scrolls are not only for Catholics, they are for mankind, and, I believe, to give us hope for the future.'

Both were immersed in deep thought. With the chime of the clock on the mantle, Alexander rose to his feet. 'I must leave you now, Dani. It is late. I'm being selfish to keep you from your rest,' he added with the first smile Dani had seen on his face in hours. 'You'll need all your strength to cope with my lively Maria.'

At the door, Dani cautioned Alex to button his coat against the chill of the night. 'Your concern touches me, Dani,' he said hoarsely. The warm Latin voice compelled Dani to caress his cheek gently. She closed her eyes against the pain and longed to be mirrored in his. He brought his lips to hers and let them linger there. Before she opened her eyes again, he was gone into the velvety night.

Ten

Where had the morning gone? Dani glanced at the Gucci watch on her slender wrist: twelve thirty. The phone shrilled, startling her. Reaching out for the receiver before it could ring a second time, Dani managed to trip over Bismarck and bruise her shin all at the same time. The receiver cradled on her shoulder, she gasped, 'Hello.'

'Dani, this is Stash. Now look, don't get alarmed but someone ransacked your apartment. I went up there today like I said I would and the place was a shambles. I did the best I could, but you know me. Two left feet and two left hands. I want to know if there was anything valuable you left behind and how will I know if there is something missing?'

'Stash, you aren't joking, are you?' Dani asked in alarm.

'Would I joke about a thing like that? Come on, Dani, you know me better than that. Listen, are you in some kind of trouble? Does it have something to do with the kid? If so, tell me and maybe I can help.

That's what friends are for, you know.'

For five seconds, Dani debated whether she should tell him or not. A vision of an angry dark-eyed Latin invaded her thoughts and helped her make a rapid decision.

'No, Stash, I'm not in any kind of trouble. Please believe me,' Dani pleaded as she crossed her fingers childishly. 'It must have been some kind of burglar or some kids. I've been lucky so far. What I mean is, I've lived there for five years and I guess I was overdue for a ransacking. How much damage did they do? Is my furniture ruined?'

'Well they did a job, I'll say that for them. To my inexperienced eye, I would say they were looking for something. Forget your furniture. There isn't anything left but the stuffing. Even your mattress was slashed to ribbons. All the closets were emptied out and everything was strewn on the floor. They even had a go at your flowerpots. They just dumped the dirt on the floor. What do you want me to do?'

'Do you mean there isn't anything to come back to? All my beautiful things. Stash, you are telling me the truth, aren't you? Do you know how long it took me to save the eight hundred dollars to buy my sofa? Three miserable years,' Dani wailed. 'Can it be reupholstered?'

'I'm afraid not,' Stash answered gruffly. 'There isn't anything left but the frame.

That's what I've been trying to tell you. It was such a thorough job that whoever did it must have been looking for something. Something that could be hidden in the stuffing. Are you sure, Dani, that you aren't in some kind of trouble?'

'No, I'm not.'

'Do you want me to report this to the police?' He waited for her answer.

God. If she said 'no', he would know for sure that something was wrong. If she said 'yes' the police would come here and then what would Alex say? Tough! It was her furniture and her savings that bought it. When she entered into this deal with the smooth-talking Latin, she hadn't bargained on having her possessions ruined. God damn it! She had loved that deep chocolate sofa.

'By all means call them.' Dani almost smiled to herself when she heard Stash's sigh of relief. 'But do me a favor and tell them I'm out of town and can't be reached. I don't want them coming up here. The neighbors frown on having the police on your doorstep. Just tell them I asked you to check the apartment from time to time. And, no, you don't know when I'll be back. Will you do it?'

'Of course I'll do it. What a dumb thing to say. I'll do the best I can. Anything else?'

'Can't think of a thing. If I do, I'll give you

189

a call. By the way did you have the phone disconnected?'

'I took care of it yesterday. You have to give them three days' notice when you want it back on. Remember that.'

'I will. And Stash, thanks for everything. I owe you one for this.'

'Sure you do. The Super Bowl game, remember. We have a date.'

'The only thing that would make me break that date would be my wedding, and then I'm not sure I wouldn't cancel the wedding. It's a date. January 2000. I wrote down the date. Be sure to call me if there is any more news, like the police finding out who did it or if the insurance company wants to pay me a fortune. Thanks again, Stash.'

Dani sat down on the maple chair with a thump. 'Now what, Danielle Arnold, private citizen,' she muttered. And, Danielle Arnold, what happens to private citizens? They get it in the neck every time, she thought cynically. I wonder how much money I actually have tied up in the furniture. 'A couple of years' salary,' she snorted. 'Did you hear that, Bismarck? We have been rendered homeless as of this day, or was it last night? I bet they even had a go at your wicker bed.' Bismarck sprang from his resting place under the kitchen table and started to spit and snarl. 'I didn't say they ruined it, I just said I wouldn't be surprised if they did.

'My God! I must be cracking up. I never thought I would see the day that I would apologize to a cat.

'What do you think, Bismarck? Should I call Alex and tell him what's happened ? Or should I forget it and pretend it was a bunch of kids out for a night of fun? Well?' she demanded. 'I've had it,' Dani screeched, as she banged her fist on the smooth surface of the round wooden table. 'Enough is enough. I loved that sofa. I'm going to tell him to pay up and cancel our ... arrangement. Let him take care of his own daughter. First he wants my life and then it's my furniture.'

Bismarck tilted his head at an angle and stared at the irate girl. In a flash, he was in her lap purring contentedly.

'Do you know something, Bismarck. I have come to the conclusion that you, too, are a male chauvinist. So hit the road,' Dani said in a decidedly miffed tone.

The big tom sniffed and walked disdainfully over to the corner and lowered himself gracefully into a round ball. He licked his whiskers nonchalantly and immediately closed his eyes.

'That's it, cop out. You and every other male in this whole damn universe. That's your answer. Take the easy way out and let women run the world.' Tears smarted Dani's eyes at the thought.

Should I call Alex or not, she wondered nastily. No, but the next time I see him, I'll tell him. 'Do you hear that, Bismarck?' Bismarck, busy grooming himself, ignored her question.

What did it all mean? Fear crept up Dani's spine, forcing her to grip the table edge to stop the trembling in her hands and arms. What if she and the child had been in the apartment? What would have happened? The oily, unctuous voice on the phone was all too clear in her mind. Would they, whoever they were, realize that the apartment was no longer inhabited? Would they find some way to follow her here? Was the child safe here in her parents' house? The house that always seemed like an impregnable fortress? Would she herself be safe?

Terror cloaked her slender body as she paced the kitchen. Up one side and down the other. Should she get a gun? It was a thought that often plagued her back in the city. With her luck, she would end up shooting herself in the leg. She had to do something. She needed some kind of defense against them. Them! If I ever get my hands on them, I'll kill the lot of them. There was no reason on this whole earth why anyone should have to live in fear and dread as she was doing. And the child. How long could she keep her feelings under wraps? Would she notice? Of course she would. She was intelligent beyond her years. Perhaps I should ask Stash to come up here and stay with us. He would come in a minute if I asked him.

I refuse to be intimidated, Dani thought. There is no way that some oily, deadly voice is going to make me cringe and be afraid to go outside the door. Alex will have to do something. He will have to do it for his child, not for me. I can take care of myself. But Maria is only a child. She has to be taken care of. And Alex, as her father, will have to see to it.

The question was: would he?

Eleven

Dani was idly snipping dried fronds from her drooping asparagus fern when Maria catapulted into the kitchen screaming, 'Papa's here.'

Dani emerged from the kitchen, scissors in one hand and a watering-can in the other. Nodding slightly and smiling at Maria's obvious joy, she acknowledged Alex's presence.

'Ladies,' Alex smiled, seeing Maria thrilled at having him refer to her as a 'lady', 'I have come to take you to the zoo. Will that be agreeable to both of you? You didn't have anything planned for the day, did you?'

Dani noticed how explicity he had stipulated 'both of you' and smiled even brighter.

'No, Papa,' Maria assured him, 'We were just going to sit around today. Weren't we, Dani?' she gurgled.

'Yes, that's what we were going to do, just sit around,' Dani laughed, waving the scissors and watering-can significantly. 'Well, whatever I was going to do in the kitchen can wait. I'm sure of that! Just give me a few minutes to straighten up and get dressed.'

'Maria can do the kitchen while you get dressed,' Alex said, urging Maria with a wink. He looked at his watch. 'Ten minutes,' he ordered.

Dani's heart raced at the thought of an outing with the tall, handsome Latin. Hours, just to be with him. Quickly, she changed into an attractive dark blue pants suit. The delicate white hand-stitching on the collar and cuffs brought out the dull sheen on the carved ivory buttons. She nodded approvingly as she sketchily applied some make-up.

Fastening wide ivory hoops in her ears, she cast a last anxious look into the mirror. There should be no complaints. She hadn't realized how the sooty air of the city had affected her complexion. But since moving here to the country her skin positively glowed. Or was it just the expectation of an outing with Alex and Maria?

Still, what did the man like? Perhaps he liked his women with more sophistication, dripping with jewelry and sleek tight hair-dos. Tough, that wasn't her style and he would have to like her the way she was.

As Dani emerged from the bedroom, she caught Alex glancing at his watch. 'Right on time, Dani,' he smiled. 'I have never known a woman as punctual as you.'

Dani smiled her expression of thanks, but her mind was still hearing the way he said her name, softly, endearingly, or was it only that subtly attractive accent that made her pulse race?

'Papa, that is not true. I am always on time. I have never made you wait for me,' Maria shouted.

'True, little one, but you did not hear me. I said "woman" and you have a way to go till you can qualify for that title.'

'You're right, Papa,' Maria said happily. 'Where did you say you were taking us?'

'To the Bronx Zoo, where else?' He laughed into Dani's eyes.

'Will we have peanuts to feed the elephants and can we have as many treats as we want?' the jubilant child asked.

'Why not? Consider it "Ladies' Day". Anything your heart desires, Maria. You also, Dani,' Alex said meaningfully, as he watched the color rise in Dani's face. 'Anything,' he repeated.

Furious at the feelings that swept through her and at the telltale blush that suffused her cheeks, she blurted, 'Then I guess I want to see the monkey cage first, have two jellied apples, one cotton candy and three hot dogs. In that order please,' she laughed, hoping her silly demands had given her enough time to recover her emotions.

Maria, never still for a moment, popped

up over the back seat to kiss her father's ear from time to time and gush her happiness during the ride.

'Have you ever been to the zoo, Dani?' There it was again, her name on his lips.

'Many times,' Dani answered. 'However, I never went there with such dignified escorts.'

'She means us, Papa! We are dignified, are we not?'

'I think so, little one,' Alex answered fondly.

'But that's good! Perhaps they will roll out a red carpet for us. What do you think, Dani?'

'I wouldn't count on it, honey,' she laughed. 'You're just another person when you get to the zoo. Only the animals are important there.'

Ninety minutes later, Alex maneuvered the long, low car into a parking space. He paid the attendant and the trio strolled into the zoo grounds.

They walked for hours. Exclaiming and oohing and aahing at the animals and their antics. Maria was ecstatic at the cleverness of the chimpanzees. Munching on a candy apple, she stood in rapt admiration at their talents.

'Truthfully, Dani, I do not think they are half as intelligent as Bismarck. Did I tell you that, Papa?'

Alex smiled and acquiesced that Bismarck was far and above the most intelligent animal he had ever seen. 'Maria, why don't you walk around for a while? Dani and I are getting tired. We'll be over here on the bench. Here is some money to buy souvenirs so that you remember your trip.' Maria scampered away as Alex and Dani sat down.

Dani watched Maria, a look of anxiety on her face. Alex, noticing, soothed her. 'Don't worry so much, Dani. The child needs some freedom, she needs to feel a bit independent. Nothing bad will happen – no one knows we're here.'

Thoughts of the ransacked apartment flashed through Dani's mind for the tenth time. She was tempted to tell Alex about the break-in but changed her mind. Her eyes quickly scanned the tanned, handsome features, the face that was beginning to mean more and more to her. It was clear that Alex was enjoying this outing to the zoo. Surely, if she told him what Stash had found in her New York apartment that narrow line would reappear between his heavy arched brows. Today, for the first time he had seemed genuinely happy and relaxed. Not for anything would Dani destroy that easy, contented expression. No, this wasn't the time to tell him, there would be another time. She would have to bear the burden for the both of them – for today anyway – and Alex was right after all: no one knew of their plans to come to the zoo. Maria would be perfectly safe.

'She is tireless,' Alex apologized for Maria. 'At times, I feel sorry for you, Dani. How-ever in the world do you manage with her?'

Dani tilted her head to the left and laughed. 'But you see, that's the whole thing. I don't manage her. She manages me! After the third day, I had to give up. We manage quite well together, as you can see.'

Alex nodded solemnly. 'It is good that you were able to become friends. Maria has not had a happy life, as you know. The fact that she manages as well as she does has never ceased to amaze me.

'There was a time,' he said soberly, 'when I thought I might lose her. Valerie has me over a barrel at the moment. I am not proud that I gave in to her demands. There was just no other way. It was a question of sur-vival for Maria.'

Almost absently, he continued to speak. 'Valerie had come to me in my study and told me what she had done to Maria. Actu-ally, she did nothing physical ... that time, it was what she did to Maria mentally. Val couldn't wait to tell me how she cowed the child. I swear to you, Dani, you will not believe me when I tell you what Valerie did.'

'Tell me, Alex,' Dani said softly.

'Yes, I think it is time you know these things. What I am about to tell you is information Valerie herself told me and the rest ... Maria was very ill, she was running a fever of one hundred and five. She was delirious when she rambled about these things. It was the eve of Maria's sixth birthday and the child was outside on the patio reading a book, Winnie the Pooh, I believe,' Alex said almost absently, his eyes staring off into the distance. 'Any other mother would have been proud if their child could read at the age of six. Not Valerie. She taunted the child and called her names. Then she threatened the child with boarding school. She told her she would be sent to Buenos Aires and would only come home on holidays. The child was terrified at the mere thought of being sent away. Valerie told her if she didn't willingly agree to go with her, she would divorce me and ask for custody of the child. It was all a threat on Valerie's part. She wanted her own way in all things. Her threats to Maria were just that, threats. She never had any interest in the child from the day she was born. She knew that if she did sue me for divorce, the judge in Argentina would give her custody of the child. I couldn't let that happen. So, I gave in,' Alex said wearily. 'I gave her everything she wanted. I think at that point I would have sold my soul to the

200

devil to be rid of her.'

'What ... what did she want?' Dani quavered.

'She wanted an unlimited checking account, her own charge accounts in all the New York stores. With the bills sent to me. She wanted to be free. Free but not divorced. I was never to ask questions. She would come and go as she pleased. I gave her everything she asked for. I paid the rent on a luxurious apartment in New York where she told me she entertained her lovers. I did everything she asked; for Maria. Now do you see why Valerie must never get her hands on the child? She only wants Maria now so she can bargain. And to hurt me. She knows how much I love the child.'

'Alex, you said she didn't hurt Maria that time. Did she physically hurt her at some other time?' Dani asked hesitantly.

'Dear God, yes,' Alex said in an agonized voice. 'She hit her on the ear. The child had to be taken to the hospital. The surgeon said it was a miracle that she saved her hearing. The surgeon himself told me that Maria talked in her delirium. That is how I found out. Maria herself was afraid to tell me for fear of the threats that Valerie made to her. Please Dani, I do not want to talk about it.' Dani nodded understandingly.

Alex's voice had turned so soft at the end of his remembrance that Dani had to strain to hear him. 'That's terrible!' Dani said, shocked beyond belief. 'It isn't that I don't believe you, Alex, I do, I ... I just can't comprehend a mother reacting that way over her own child. It ... it's unholy! That poor child. And to look at her you'd think she'd never had one unhappy day in her life.'

'Thanks to you, Dani, Maria has never been so happy. She is completely different. She says she loves you more than Anna, and that is quite a lot,' Alex laughed.

'Alex, I want your promise that none of this ... this thing with Valerie will ever affect Maria.' She looked into Alex's eyes and found no answer there.

'Well?' Dani repeated.

'I will do whatever has to be done, Dani. You may call it fate, destiny, whatever. I can change nothing at this time. I must do what I have to do. Say no more, Querida, I do not want this day to be marred with your anger. I know what I am doing, you will have to trust me.'

Maria scampered back to them, her arms full of small packages. 'I almost bought out the store. And I have sixty-four cents left,' she announced proudly.

'You are a most astute shopper, Maria,' Alex laughed. 'Let us hope that the recipients will be overjoyed with these tantalizing gifts.

'I think we should be getting back, don't you, Dani?' There it was again, the sound of her name on his lips causing her to tingle. It was her name, she had heard it a thousand times, written it a million. But there was something in his tone, when he said 'Dani'. Something of a caress.

'Yes, it's getting late and Maria has been up till all hours every night this week.'

'Would you like to stop for dinner on the way home?'

'Heavens no! I couldn't eat a thing. Besides,' Dani said holding her stomach, 'three chili dogs and cotton candy don't go together very well.'

'But Dani, I ate the same thing and I also had pizza and a jellied apple and there is nothing wrong with my stomach!' Maria giggled.

'That's because yours is made of cast iron.'

'It would appear that you have been outvoted, Maria,' Alex laughed. 'So it is home for now. Perhaps another time you lovely ladies will give me the honor of your company for dinner.'

'Just say when, Papa,' Maria giggled as she settled back on the bench.

On the ride home, Maria napped and Alex and Dani sat quietly, each lost in their own thoughts. After seeing them into the house, Alex said, 'I must be on my way. Thank you for spending such an enjoyable day with me.' His eyes penetrated deeply, questioning.

She supposed he was worried that what he had said about Valerie had spoiled the day for Dani.

'I had a lovely time, Alex,' she reassured him, smiling into his dark luminous eyes. 'I know Maria did.'

'Good night, Querida, and you too, little one.'

Twelve

Alexander Mendeneres left the large, old house on Hollow Road and when he left he removed, if not bodily then spiritually, a part of Dani that would be forever his.

If Dani was more quiet and serious, there was no one to notice. Maria and the boys were intent on their own fun-filled days. For the most part, the evenings were spent watching television and waiting for the phone to ring. For the time being, Dani would be content just to hear Alex's voice.

It was the middle of October, one of those rare Indian summer days. Maria's emergency haircut had lengthened a bit and waved about her head in beguiling, soft curls, bringing the shimmering brown eyes into prominence.

They were raking the brilliant autumn leaves into a huge pile to be burned that evening when, finally unable to stand it a moment longer, Dani looked down and demanded bluntly, 'Tell me of your mother, Maria.' As soon as the words were spoken, she wished they hadn't been uttered. The small face clouded, but the words rushed out as though a dam had finally broken.

'My mother is very beautiful. Everyone says so. But she is not beautiful inside like my grandmother and Papa, and you, too, Dani. She doesn't love me.' At Dani's stricken look, she hastened to add, 'It is so. She told me herself. My mother said I ruined her figure and that I was an ugly child. My mother also hates my father. He did everything to make my mother happy. My grandmother said he spent a fortune on clothes and jewels for her. My mother would ask what good they were when there were only peasants to see her wearing them. All my mother did was scream at my father. He would look so sad all the time. Then one day my Papa was talking to my grandmother in the library...'

Maria's voice held a faint tremor and her face drew into downcast lines. Dani knew that Maria would never fully come to grips with her situation if she didn't confide in someone. Through Maria's words and expressions, Dani was drawn deeper into the web of the child's misery.

'I was going down our mosaic corridor on my way to the library when I saw my mother eavesdropping at the door. She grabbed my arm and shook me till I thought my teeth would rattle. She called me a little sneak and said I gave her the creeps. It was she who was doing the sneaking.' Maria's face was rigid with fear as she recalled the scene. 'I told her I was only going to the library for a book. Then when she became more upset, I asked her why she was listening at the door. She said I was a liar and that she wasn't listening at the door. I told her it was a sin to tell a lie and that I saw her. Oh Dani, her face was so hateful,' Maria shuddered.

'Honey, I'm sorry I asked you. I can see it upsets you to talk about it. Why don't we forget it for now? Perhaps some other time when you feel more up to it.'

Maria didn't seem to hear Dani's voice for she continued, 'That is when she hit me. A fierce blow to the side of the head. I fell and tried to clear my head but everything was blurred. I could barely see. I sat crouched on the floor and my mother stared down at me. I was so afraid. She told me that if I said even one word to my father of what happened she would take me away and I would never see Papa and my grandmother again. I did not say "yes" and I did not say "no". My head hurt so bad I could not talk. When I did not answer her, she kicked me in the side with the toe of her sandal. I almost threw up, Dani – that's how bad the pain was. Then I saw my father come out of the study just as I noticed a shadow start to form in the corner of the hall. The Monk was coming to help me, but when he saw my father he went away. He knew my father would take care of me.'

'Good Lord,' Dani exclaimed. 'Did you tell your father how she abused you?'

Maria shook her head, the dark curls bobbing. 'I would not tell, I thought she would do what she said – take me away. I would die, if I did not have my Papa,' Maria said simply. 'Anyway, my mother pretended that she had just arrived, that I was running down the hall and tripped and fell, striking my head on the doorway. Then my mother told another lie. She said I was running from the Monk. That was when I could see that Papa knew she was lying. I would never run from the Monk. The Monk protects me.'

'Then what happened?' Dani asked breathlessly.

'Papa carried me to bed and asked me what happened. I lied to him, Dani,' Maria said defensively. 'That was the only time I ever told Papa a lie. I told him I was all right. I almost died of fright when my mother pretended concern and said she would stay with me. She said I just had a bad fright and I needed rest. She said she would stay with me till I fell asleep. My papa was upset, but grandmother led him away and said my mother was right, I needed rest.'

'Maria, you should have told your father.

He would have known what to do.'

'I was afraid. I did not like the look in my mother's eyes at that moment. After everyone left, she said I had done well and she was proud of me. I lay very quiet and prayed that she would go away. She did not. She just kept standing by my bed and watching me. Then all of a sudden, she grabbed one of my curls and wound it around her finger. At first, I thought she was just touching my hair like grandmother does sometimes. That is not what she was doing. She twisted my hair and pulled it with all her might. I truly thought my head was going to come off. Then I knew I had to play the trick because I could not stand the pain and, in truth, I could not stand to look at my mother.'

'What trick did you play?'

'I pretended I saw the Monk. I hope Brother Gian will one day forgive me. But I did not know what else to do. I started to cry and whine, you know the way little children do. I said that Mama did not mean to hurt me and to spare her. I said a lot of things that I do not remember now. She demanded to know what I was babbling about. I just kept my eyes on the corner of the room and kept talking. I just said whatever popped into my head. At first it was the trick, then it was real. The room started to get dark, very slowly at first, and the draperies moved in the breeze that came from nowhere. The wind became stronger and my mother's hair was blowing wildly as were her skirts. The wind was only centered around her. She ran screaming from the room saying I was demented and she would take steps to have me locked away.'

'Oh you poor baby,' Dani crooned, clutching the child to her breast. 'How you must have suffered. If only you had told your father.'

'I guess I fell asleep then, for when I woke,' Maria said to a misty-eyed Dani, 'I tried my best to be brave, but the pain in my ear was so bad all I did was cry.'

Dani could picture the brave little girl lying exhausted and white upon her pillow.

'I wondered how badly I was hurt,' Maria said matter-of-factly, 'because I could not hear anything at all. It was strange, Dani, my own voice sounded husky and far away to me. I stayed in bed, hoping no one would know how badly my ear hurt. But I became very ill and Papa took me to the hospital. I think my father knows what really happened. Sometimes I would see him looking at me as if he knew I had told a lie. I asked one of the doctors at the hospital if I talked when I was sick. He said quite cheerfully that I did not shut up for five minutes. But I did not mean for him to know.'

'If he does, I'm sure that he understands. Your Papa is a very wise man. Maria, tell me more of the Monk of Mendeneres.'

'The Mendeneres Monk is Brother Gian. They say he was a scribe to a heavenly angel. He was put into a dungeon and suffered greatly. Doctor Mendeneres, an ancestor of mine, befriended him when no one else would help him. That is why he protects the Mendeneres. He watches over us, so nothing evil will happen. My mother is evil. The Monk knows this. Many times when she is near me, I see his shadow. The Monk is the only thing that my mother is afraid of. She knows she is not a true Mendeneres. Do not think because he let Valerie hit me that he was not protecting me. He only comes when I want him. It is a sort of mental thing. If I cannot handle the situation then he comes. I do not call him for every little thing. It must be important. He knows I was not really playing the trick. I needed him desperately.'

Dani blinked. Who was she to dispute the child? Her blood boiled for this faceless woman. Quickly she gathered the child to her and hugged her.

'Try not to mind too much, Maria. Your father loves you dearly, as do I and your grandmother.'

'Do you know the secret?'

'No, Maria, I do not,' Dani lied. The child had enough to bear without adding that to her other list of things to worry about.

'That is why she left,' Maria said. 'My mother heard my Papa and grandmother. Now she knows the secret. Dani, I don't want to go back to Argentina. Can't I stay here with you? Could you adopt me? I will help you all I can. I'm small and I don't take up much room and, since Danny said that I was getting fat, I will diet and not eat much food. Please, Dani, can I stay with you?'

Shocked, Dani stared at the child, her jaw dropping. 'But what of your father? Think how he will feel if you don't return with him. He loves you Maria, more than life itself. He told me so.'

'I know that,' the child said pathetically. 'But I do not want to go back, I want to stay here. Could you marry my father?' she asked seriously.

'Maria,' Dani said softly, 'you know that is impossible. You must learn that there are many things in this life that can't be changed and that we have to accept things and situations for what they are. I told you it was all part of growing up. I would truly love to have you live with me, but that can't be. We're only together now because I'm helping your father. Right now he has some problems that he has to solve. When he has completed his task, I'll have to return to the city and my job. I hope you understand. I told you once before that it was all right to dream, but that reality had to set in sooner or later. Perhaps, in a few years' time, I can come to Argentina on a vacation and see you. By then, you'll be a teenager and quite grown up.' Dani looked at the child and knew she understood the words for what they were.

'While you were sleeping last night, I called my father. I told him that I did not want to return to Argentina with him and that I wanted to stay here with you.'

'Maria, you didn't?' Shocked, Dani could only stare at the wide-eyed child.

'I will run away if I have to go back. I will not go,' the child said stubbornly.

'Maria, what did your father say?'

'He said nothing, Dani. He did not answer me.'

'I should think so. You probably shocked him speechless. Maria, that was a very thoughtless thing for you to do. Think how he must feel. He loves you so much. You must have hurt him very deeply.'

'I don't care. I have been hurt many times. No one cares when I am hurt.'

'Maria, I don't think that's true. Your mother has hurt you. Not your father. You can't take your frustrations out on the one person who loves you above all else. Poor baby,' Dani crooned, holding the child close to her. 'These are the years when you need a mother the most, and I fear I am a poor substitute. Listen to me, Maria, you love

213

me, I understand that, and I love you, too. This ... this feeling that you have about wanting to stay here with me is a result of ... of not having a real mother like Kelly and the boys do, but you have something just as good. You have a father who loves you. I'm not saying that the boys' fathers don't love them, but it is in a different way. Your father has had to be both a mother and father to you even when your mother was in Argentina. I am sure that he has spent more time with you than any of the boys' fathers do with them. I don't think I'm explaining this very well,' Dani said pitifully. 'I guess one of the reasons is that I'm not a mother.'

'Oh, Dani, how I wish you were my mother,' the child said sadly.

And I wish it were so myself, Dani thought.

Alexander Mendeneres stood quietly by a huge boxwood shrub and listened with aching heart to the words of his daughter. He listened in amazement at the tall, lovely girl's words as she praised him. He drew his eyes into slits and peered at the sun. He looked around the quiet yard and at the lush pile of brilliant leaves. Again, he looked at this stunning American woman who had returned his kiss so passionately. No, she wasn't a girl. She was a woman. Was this mission of his worthwhile? He now had some small, yet serious, doubts. His mind

214

was weary and so was his body. All he wanted was to be left in peace and be able to return to his country and to fulfill his mission. Suddenly, he felt like a fool standing hiding and spying behind a shrub. He should have known that Dani would take care of the situation. He was just about to turn and leave when Maria spotted him.

'Papa,' she screeched and ran to him. 'Oh, I am so sorry I said what I did. Truly, I love you, more than anyone in this whole world. Oh, Papa, I am so sorry. Dani has explained everything to me.'

Alexander Mendeneres cradled his only daughter to him and sought Dani's eyes. They stared at one another, holding each other's gaze – Dani's full of tears and Alexander's full of love and longing.

Unable to keep her gaze locked on him, Dani bent down to pick up the rake to resume cleaning the yard. A large, glistening tear fell on her hand. When she looked up again he was gone and Maria was waving at the car as it backed out of the driveway.

'I have an idea,' Dani said with forced brightness. 'Let's picnic. It will be good for both of us. We can finish the yard tomorrow.'

'I would like a picnic,' Maria cried happily. As the limousine drew away, a sporty compact pulled in. 'It's Stash, can he go with us?'

'Why not?'

'Hiya, ladies,' Stash called.

Maria threw herself into his burly arms, crushing against his body and squealing, 'We are going on a picnic and you are coming.'

'Next to beautiful girls, there's nothing I like better.'

'Come on, I'll get the basket,' Dani laughed. 'You can help me, Maria.'

'I'll help,' Stash volunteered.

'Oh no you won't, that kitchen isn't big enough for the three of us. Sit down and we'll be ready in ten minutes.'

Stash grumbled, good-naturedly, and lumbered into the living-room. He sought out his favorite chair next to the hearth and, as always, whenever he visited, felt the pervading peace of the cottage surround him. It was a place where a man could kick off his shoes, put up his feet and belong; if one could belong to a house. As with most men, the sofa's muted colors as well as the rest of the room escaped his eyes. His appreciation was sensory. The soft leather of the deep chair was soft and yielding beneath him. The faint aroma of long dead fires misted toward him, surrounded him with a feeling of ease and good living. It was a place for all time.

Dani stuck her head in the door. 'Let's go, we have enough food here for an army. I hope you're hungry.'

'I'm starved,' Stash laughed as he grabbed Maria in one arm and the bulging picnic basket in the other. 'Let's go!'

Alex stood outside his wife Valerie's apartment door, with his hand poised to knock. He hesitated a moment, gathering his wits. When he had left the little house in the country, he had driven at break-neck speed, unmindful of the traffic. When he heard Maria profess her love for Dani and reveal the cruelty which Val had employed against her, his blood boiled. His conscience pursued him along the highways until he found himself here, just a wooden panel away from the object of his daughter's fears.

Thoughts flashed through his mind and he was aware of his wrongdoing, his part in the whole scenario. How could he have been deceived by Valerie? Had her beauty been so overwhelming that he had been blind to her selfishness? He acknowledged the stark, naked facts and they hurt, cutting him, as if he were bleeding. He had waited long enough, played the game too well. Now he must dash everything and, for Maria's sake, confront Valerie and make her understand that under no conditions would she gain their child.

How valiant his thoughts seemed, how humble, how chagrined when he forced himself to admit he would do anything and everything possible to gain those scrolls even at a deep, personal loss to himself. Perhaps, ultimately, the loss of Maria herself. Yet, now there was doubt that, once he had retrieved the scrolls, he would move heaven and earth to keep his daughter. As he rapped sharply on the door, the dark recrimination-filled eyes of Dani Arnold flashed before him.

The door swung and Valerie stood with her back to the soft lamplight, amazement written on her face. 'Alex, what are you doing here? I thought I told you I'd get in touch with you!'

'You did, Val, but this has gone on long enough.' He advanced on her, forcing her to move backward into the apartment.

'Get out of here, Alex, get out now!'

'Not this time, Val. I've already spent too much of my life doing your bidding. Now it's your turn to listen to me!'

His eyes hopscotched around the apartment and he was glad that Eugene was nowhere to be found.

Val placed herself brazenly in front of him, allowing her perfectly penciled mouth to draw into a sneer. 'That's right, Alex, he isn't here. Isn't that what you were afraid of? That he'll help me?'

Her snide tone infuriated Alex even more, and he roared, 'You underestimate me,

Valerie. I'm not afraid of Eugene. Remember how many times I've bailed him out of a scrape because he's spineless. I know Eugene's weakness too well ever to be afraid of him.'

'So I suppose you came over here to try and muscle me out of the scrolls. Well, it won't work, Alex! I'll never tell you where they are. Never!'

He grabbed her arm and squeezed till it hurt, the pain registering on her face. 'I think you will, Val,' he said in a calm, modulated voice that was geared to a key turning in the lock. He wasn't surprised to see Eugene enter the room.

'Alex, I hope I'm not interrupting some touching reconciliation scene.' Eugene's too long, straight, fair hair hung over one eye. His sarcastic, droll mouth forced itself into a broad, malicious grin.

Valerie's eyes darted from one man to the other. The tip of her pink tongue licked at her upper lip. The slight action did not go unnoticed by Alex, nor did he miss the triumphant look in her eyes.

'No, Eugene, nothing could be farther from the truth and, as for you, Val, don't get your hopes up that Eugene and I will fight over you. Eugene has more sense than that. Don't you, Eugene?'

The tall, sandy-haired man appeared decidedly uncomfortable. He stretched his neck as though he were trying to free it from an overly tight collar.

'I've told Val and now I'll tell you, I'm not through playing these games. I'm prepared to pay for the scrolls.'

Eugene advanced on Val and menacingly swung her around. 'You little bitch! You told him, didn't you? You told him the deal fell through for the scrolls. Don't lie to me, admit it!'

Valerie was astonished by this sudden attack. 'No, I swear, I didn't say anything. He just came here knocking on the door and I thought you had forgotten your key.'

Eugene was hard put to control himself till Alex placed a restraining hand on his shoulder. 'That's enough.'

Valerie shot a look of hatred at her husband. 'It's true. The deal did fall through on those stupid scrolls. The only person in the world who could possibly want them is you, Alex.'

'And what are you prepared to pay for them?' Eugene broke in.

'Yes, what are you prepared to pay, Alex? Your mother's jewels, your fine house and hacienda? Your life?' Her eyes glittered greedily. 'Maria?'

'Stop it, Valerie,' Eugene warned. His mind was reeling at the thought of Alex's wealth, his Latin determination to regain the scrolls. Val noted her brother's attempt to interfere and stopped him with a frantic hand gesture.

'Don't stop me, Eugene!' Then putting herself close to Alex, she whined, 'Just what *are* you willing to pay? And just what are you paying for, Alex? My lost youth? The years I rotted away in your house? The insults I've suffered because of your mother? You couldn't allow me to be a part of your secret, could you? No, only your mother, the grande dame.'

Alex saw the greed and hatred in her eyes. He knew then that Valerie would settle for nothing less than seeing him ruined. She knew he'd give anything for the ancient parchments.

For the first time, Eugene sensed that Val had been right all along. Alex appeared so determined to have his way that he would face ruin rather than lose the scrolls. Eugene moistened his lips in anticipation of the profit he would gain by playing Alex's game, but now Valerie was going too far. If he allowed it, she would lose any chance she had of getting her hands on the Mendeneres' fortune, which danced before his eyes.

Alex studied Valerie carefully. Virulence glistened in her eyes. He saw the calculated figuring taking place inside her head. The money was secondary, in fact, Alex would bet that the money was Eugene's idea, not Valerie's. All she wanted was to see Alex ruined, financially, morally, emotionally.

Valerie smiled, revealing her sharp, small white teeth. 'You'd even trade off Maria, wouldn't you?'

Now the game was clear. It wasn't the money. That would hurt him, but not enough. It was his child she wanted. She knew that this way his destruction would be complete. He gathered himself to full height and looked down into her glittering green eyes. His answer was too long in coming for Valerie. She wanted to know now!

'Wouldn't you! You'd even trade off Maria!'

'If necessary,' came his soft reply. Quickly, Alex turned on his heel and left the apartment, leaving two enraged people in his wake.

He stepped out into the hall and moved toward the elevator. Perspiration broke out on his brow and upper lip. He no longer felt controlled, calm, and he could taste bile rising up in his mouth. 'Good God,' he prayed, 'let me have done the right thing. Help me to keep Maria and gain the scrolls.'

The taste in his mouth became more bitter and he willed his gut to settle itself and be strong for what he had to do next.

Halloween started out as a dismal day. The sky was overcast, the day raw and cold. Fortunately, the weather did not dampen the children's spirits. All day, they gave out hints to each other on the costumes they were going to wear that night. Maria was ecstatic. After two hours of trick or treating, there was to be a party at the Alperts' house. Dani had spent the previous day baking gingerbread and had driven two miles up the road to buy cider and the huge apples that were to be her contribution to the night's festivities.

Sarah Alpert had invited Dani to a more sophisticated party that would start after the children were tucked away, but she knew a polite, quick appearance would be all that she'd make. A party was no fun without an escort. Sensing Dani's reluctance, Sarah volunteered her brother but she rejected the offer saying she wanted to finish a chapter on the cookbook.

Of late, that cookbook had covered a multitude of excuses. If the truth were known, she detested the whole idea. She could no longer get into the swing of things. The household chores completed, Dani would sit by the hour and dream impossible dreams. Playing sad songs on the stereo, and smoking incessantly was another favorite pastime.

By seven thirty, Maria was dressed as 'the Batman' and raring to go. She marched out to the corner and stood under the tulip tree to wait for the others to join her.

Thirteen

'Dani, I had the best time ever.'

Dani smiled as she looked at the pudgy Batman with drooping eyes, clutching a plastic bag containing two swinging goldfish. 'Let's get you undressed and into bed. Just wash your face. The candy apples and the chocolate cake must have been good.'

'How did you know we ate that?'

'Let's just call it an educated guess.'

As Dani waited for Maria to shed her beloved costume, she listened to a steady flow of sleepy talk. 'Dunking for apples ... wet spaghetti and pealed grapes ... Lori didn't come ... Batman too ... mother upset ... everyone is looking...'

Dani's scalp prickled, 'Did I hear you right, Maria? Lori didn't go to the party?'

'I guess she changed her mind,' came the sleepy response.

'I thought you said everyone was looking for her. Do you mean she's lost?'

Maria nodded sleepily.

'But that's terrible. Who's looking for her? Do you know?'

Another nod. 'All the fathers are out looking. So are Kelly and Tony. Their fathers said they were old enough and knew the woods as well as the men, if not better.'

Dani looked at the sleepy child fighting to keep her eyes open. Quickly, she tucked her in and, before she could kiss her goodnight, Maria was breathing steadily. How beautiful, Dani thought fondly. Smiling at the close, cropped hair and the thick, velvety eyelashes, she turned off the lamp and tip-toed from the room.

With trembling hands, Dani dialed the Alperts' number. The phone rang only once. 'This is Dani,' she said to the alert voice on the other end.

'I thought it might be you. I suppose Maria told you about Lori's disappearance.'

'What happened? Do you know?'

'Just what her mother told me. She dressed Lori as Batman and walked her to the tulip tree to meet the rest of the children, as you know. Ann Jennings said she left her there at seven fifty. Kelly left here about the same time and he said she wasn't there. No one saw her all evening.'

Dani felt the fine hairs on the back of her neck move. 'It's after midnight. Where could she be?'

'God only knows, Dani. I'm worried sick. I feel like it's all my fault. It was my idea to have the party.'

While Dani made soothing noises, her mind raced. Hanging up the phone, she quickly ran and locked the doors and kitchen windows. Breathing raggedly, Dani sat down by the dying fire and willed her mind to stop reeling. Out of desperation, she leaped up and threw some logs on the dying fire embers and watched the spurt as they showered over the cherry logs. It couldn't be, could it? It had to be. What other explanation was there? Lori had been kidnapped. My God, what should she do? Could she call the police without endangering Alex's plans and possibly Maria? Would the abductors let her go when they realized their mistake, or would they hold her? God in heaven! What had she gotten herself into? Damn! Damn! Damn!

She reached for the phone and yanked it so hard the receiver fell violently against her knee.

Dani dialed Alex's number and waited. One, two ... six ... nine ... 'Yes?' came the guarded voice.

'This is Dani. I must talk to you. Something has happened.' Quickly, she recited the events of the night and waited for his reaction.

'Listen to me, Dani. Do not do anything. I swear to you that when Valerie realizes she has the wrong child, she will return your little Lori.'

'How can you be so sure? I can't just sit here and not tell the child's mother the truth. How can you be so cruel?'

'Cruelty has nothing to do with it,' came the crisp reply. 'You will have to take my word, for the child will be returned to its parents. I can do nothing at the moment. In fact, we are both helpless, aren't we?'

'Maybe you are, but I'm not,' Dani shouted at the calm Latin. 'You can't play with people's lives like you're doing. And that's what you're doing and you damn well know it.' She lowered her voice so as not to wake Maria. 'I let you maneuver us but you can't stand by and let something happen to little Lori. She's only six years old, Alex.'

'I must. Don't you see?' came the torn reply. 'I'm pleading with you, Dani. Do nothing till morning.'

'And let that child be out all night? What about her parents who are worried sick? Not on your life, Alexander Renaldo Mendeneres. I'm calling the police. I want to be able to live with myself. For all I care, you can take your daughter and all your suppressed people and jump off a bridge.' A sob caught in her throat as she hung up the phone.

Dani mixed herself a strong drink and lit a cigarette before she pulled the phone on to her lap again. She leafed through the pages for the number of the police department. The receiver in one hand, her finger poised to dial, she was startled to hear a loud knock at the door.

The phone slid to the floor as Dani raced to the door. 'Mrs Alpert! Did you find her?'

'You're still up. I thought you might be,' Sarah Alpert smiled as her eyes took in the drawn draperies and she hadn't missed hearing the chain being moved. 'I was going to call you but I thought it would be better if I told you the good news in person. They found her. She's safe and home in bed right this minute. A group of teenagers found her wandering down the streets in Flemington.'

'What happened?' Dani asked, relief written all over her face.

Sarah shrugged. 'Lori is asleep. As near as the police can figure it, some men picked her up. What I don't understand is why they let her go, unless...' she said, looking squarely at Dani, 'they had the wrong child. Lori is about Maria's build, even though she's younger. And they were both wearing the same costume. I don't understand any of it. Do you?' Involuntarily, her gaze went to the chain lock on the door, as did Dani's.

Dani shook her head. Sarah Alpert was no fool. She knew it was Maria the men were after. God, I could kill that Alex, she thought nastily.

'Well, it's late. I'll see you tomorrow. Get a good night's sleep. Maria is OK, isn't she?'

Dani nodded, her mind speeding. She

closed and locked the front door, replaced the telephone and finished her drink before she ground out the cigarette she hadn't smoked. Again, she looked at the phone. Let him simmer, she thought viciously. Why should I tell him? He doesn't deserve an explanation, even if he was right. Who did he think he was anyway? With a frenzied motion, she threw the phone book into the bright dancing flames.

She slept fitfully, one nightmare breaking on another. Alexander Renaldo Mendeneres was hung in effigy all night long. The small clock read six ten but she could never go back to sleep. Instead she plugged in the coffee pot and took a leisurely bath, purposely making her mind blank. Fortified to face the day, she opened the front door and picked up the morning paper.

Carrying her coffee into the living-room, she sat down and opened the paper. She searched the small local paper till she found what she wanted. It was only a small article but it was what she wanted.

Eight-year-old Lori Jennings was kidnapped for several hours, yet found wandering on the main street in Flemington late last evening. Police are at a loss to explain the circumstances surrounding the child's disappearance. Lori, tired and sleepy, repeatedly told police that 'the man with the earring kept saying the party had been changed'. Police are checking further into the incident.

Dani read the small paragraph a second time. Finishing her coffee and lighting another cigarette, she returned to the front page of the paper. This time she started to read with her usual thoroughness. She went from one page to the next and attacked the women's page with her usual zest. There it was: how could she have missed it the first time? Because you weren't looking for it, she answered herself. It was a picture of the strikingly beautiful woman from the airport. Dani lowered her eyes and flinched at the wording of the caption.

Valerie Camilla Mendeneres, wife of wealthy businessman Alexander Renaldo Mendeneres of Argentina, having dinner at 21 with multi-millionaire Jason Sinclair.

Dani squinted at the picture and felt sick. Lord, she was beautiful. She was as beautiful as Alex was handsome. What a striking couple they must have made, she thought jealously. If this was Valerie, then the man with her at the airport, the one with the earring, must be her brother. What did the piece mean? Jason Sinclair – the name had a familiar ring.

She let her mind have its way. Back in her research days, she had been asked to find out about and to interview an eccentric millionaire. He was a kook of the first order. He dabbled in everything. There wasn't anything he didn't have his fingers into and he was also a cultist. She looked at the unflattering picture of the flabby eccentric and grimaced. Heavy jowls, beady eyes that almost glittered, no eyebrows and a completely bald head. He had blubbery lips that seemed to sneer continually. Dani cringed as she remembered the remarks he had made to her. He thought money could buy anything, including her. He had even offered to set her up in a penthouse for her 'favors', as he so delicately put it. Dani had laughed openly and told him exactly what she thought of his 'favors'. By the time she got back to her office with her incomplete interview, she had been fired. Her personal belongings were piled helter-skelter in a box on her desk. Shrugging philosophically, she collected unemployment for a few months.

Dani looked at the picture again ... Suddenly, it all fell into place. Eccentric millionaire, it had to be. Valerie's contact. Then she grew confused remembering what Alex had said about his picture being days old when it appeared in the paper. A fill-in, he called it. Dani scoured the entire column for some mention as to the date the picture of Valerie was taken. Nothing.

She certainly is beautiful, Dani thought enviously, as she peered at the picture of Valerie Mendeneres. They must have made a handsome pair, she thought, jealously. And the child. What of the child? A mother who doesn't care one whit about her own flesh and blood, and a father who would sacrifice his own child for his own ends, whatever they may be. And here I sit, she grimaced, *schnook* of the year, taking care of their child, and no doubt caring more about her than either of them. Yes, sir, *schnook* of the year! She wadded up the paper and threw it into the fireplace. Carefully, she lit a match and watched the paper curl and turn black, then catch and spurt into flames. She continued to watch as the flames leaped and then died down. So much for Valerie Mendeneres and Jason Sinclair.

Later, furiously beating eggs with a wire whisk, Dani wished she could beat Maria's father as efficiently. He made her so angry and so ... weak in the knees. Dialing the now familiar number, she waited, taking shallow breaths. Briefly, in a trembling voice, she told him what had happened. Why did the mere sound of his voice turn her into a mass of quivering jelly? She waited for his comment. 'I told you so,' he answered in cold clipped tones. Stunned, Dani found herself speechless. Why did he do this to her? 'What kind of man are you?' she blurted.

'I believe you asked me that once before and I answered you then. I see no reason to discuss my character again,' came the imperious reply.

Dani felt outraged at his tone. It was like a devil had her tongue. 'You ... you ... male chauvinist, you ... masochist ... you ... odious, infuriating *schnook*,' she choked.

There was laughter in his voice. 'I understand all the endearing terms except the last. Explain please, Dani.'

He was laughing at her. And she was letting him. 'Look it up in the dictionary,' she snarled.

'Whatever you say,' he answered arrogantly. 'You tend to your job and I'll tend to mine.'

Dani replaced the phone and plopped down on the deep orange chair. 'I take it all back, Bismarck – you and I belong together.' A large, shimmering tear rolled down her cheek. He was insufferable. He goes back into the ninety-seven per cent. She stroked the large cat as the tears flowed down her cheeks. To think he had the ability to make her cry, to turn her into a shivering wreck. No man had ever done that to her. She hiccuped pitifully and continued to stroke the cat. 'Well, I've never been a substitute mother before.' She dumped the big tom on the floor and wiped her eyes with the dishtowel. What other reason could there be?

Alexander Mendeneres replaced the phone gently on the cradle and stared into space. Was the girl crying? If she was, he was sorry, but he had no other choice. Why didn't she try to understand? He realized how hard he must have appeared to her. His eyes closed, his face became hooded as his mind raced. The girl would do as he ordered. Hadn't he paid her an astronomical sum of money to do his bidding? Suddenly, his whirling thoughts calmed. Money would never buy Danielle Arnold. You could only have what she would be willing to give. Alex smiled, he would have it no other way.

Dani had grown to love Maria. He was sure of it and the child loved her. The lovely girl was, at the moment, like a mother lion defending her child – no, his child. He owed her something for that. He knew in his heart that she would protect his daughter with her life, if necessary. His dark eyes took on a far-away look and his muscular shoulders slumped. For a moment, he looked as defeated as he felt. Pulling his weary shoulders back, he brought his eyes into focus and reached for his jacket. He straightened his tie and glanced in the foyer mirror. Satisfied, he strode purposefully from the room.

Breakfast over, Dani was busily clearing the table when the phone shrilled. She looked at the oblong telephone and fervently hoped that the voice on the other end was Alexander's, so she could hang up on him. Picking it up, she uttered a cautious 'Hello'.

'Miss Arnold, this is Kelly. Can Maria come over to play Monopoly?'

Disappointment was heavy in her chest. 'I guess so, Kelly, but I'm not sure if she knows how to play.'

'That's OK, Miss Arnold. We'll teach her,' Kelly said cheerfully.

Dani hung up, her hands trembling. She had been so sure it would be Alexander. 'Maria,' she called. 'Kelly wants you to go over to play Monopoly. Wear your raincoat and boots. I'll walk over with you.' Fear knotted her stomach as she thought of Lori Jennings. She wouldn't let Maria out of her sight. She would also make sure Kelly and the boys understood the situation. If necessary, she would blame Alex. She only had to say that he was feeling overprotective, after hearing the news of Lori. The boys would be agreeable, she was sure of it.

'Maria, I want you to do me a favor.' At the child's happy nod, she continued. 'There appears,' she said tapping the folded newspaper, 'to be a rash of burglaries around here. I want you to promise me you won't open the door to anyone unless you know who it is.' Dani smiled at the child in case any undertones had come through.

'Gotcha,' Maria agreed solemnly. 'Dani, what is Monopoly?' she asked cautiously.

'It's a game you play with fake money. The boys will teach you. I'm going to work on my book this morning and do some practice cooking, so you run along.'

Back in the house, Dani sat down heavily on the flowered chintz chair. I really don't feel like cooking, she told herself. Well, what do you feel like doing? she asked herself. There was no answer. If she didn't feel like cooking, she could clean house. The house didn't need cleaning.

'Well, what do you want?' she wailed aloud to the empty kitchen. Bismarck jumped in outrage at the tone of his mistress. He hopped on to her lap and purred forgivingly.

'I'm going for a walk, rain and all. Maybe it will help me to think,' she muttered to him.

Dani pulled a bright slicker off the pantry door and fastened the hood on to the coat. She dug out a pair of ancient boots from the box and left by the back door.

For over an hour, she walked aimlessly. As she was trudging up the steep incline to the back of the house, a car stopped. The rain was coming down in torrents, so she could barely see the occupant. All she heard was the voice. Damn! It was the ninety-seven per cent. 'No thanks,' she said coldly, 'I prefer to walk.' The window rolled back up and the car pulled around her. Damn the man. He could have at least insisted she get in. By tomorrow, she would probably have pneumonia. He would dance on her grave. When she reached the steps to her house, Dani looked up and there he stood. In all his glory, she thought nastily. And here I stand. Like a drowned rat! 'Who cares?' she muttered under her breath.

'Well, I see you made it.'

'Did you think I wouldn't?' Dani snapped.

'It was touch and go for a while,' the man smiled. 'But I knew you'd make it. You aren't a *schnook*,' his eyes laughed at her.

Dani ignored his humorous overtures and fished her key from the cavernous raincoat pocket.

'Allow me,' Alexander Mendeneres said gallantly, taking it from her wet, cold fingers. He pressed his hand against her lower back, ushering her into her own living-room like she was going to a formal ball. Dani was irritated with the man. No, mad as hell was better. Hell, she was downright infuriated with him. The colossal nerve of the man. Tears pricked her eyes. Shedding the wet clothes by the door, she marched over to the huge fireplace and threw in some logs and some small kindling. Striking a match, she watched the dry wood leap into flame. Once more in control of herself, she turned to face the man standing next to her. 'Well,' she said coldly.

'Sit down. There's something I have to tell you.'

'I prefer to stand, thank you.'

Alexander Mendeneres looked at the tall, lovely woman and at the angry eyes, her body rigid. Their eyes locked. Both bodies moved at the same time. She fit into his arms like she belonged there. He never wanted to let her go. This strange woman, the protector of his child. He wanted her for now, for always. Their lips met and she returned his kiss as ardently as he had hoped she would. Dani's head reeled. She felt herself on a cloud and floating. As Alex clasped her face in his two hands, Dani came back to reality when she thought she heard murmured words. It sounded like Alex said, 'God help us both.'

Fourteen

Dani walked into the bathroom to gather up the dirty laundry. Her rubber-soled tennis shoes crunched on the grit from Bismarck's litter box. Her gaze swiveled around the small room – there was kitty litter plus Bismarck's personal droppings all over the floor. Not only was it all over the floor, but there was a clear print of a child's sneaker in a soft mass, now squelched between the tiles.

Aaghh! She gulped as she beat a hasty retreat back to the living-room. 'Miserable kid. I told her not to leave until she took care of the litter box. One of her endearing traits.' She mashed her teeth together. 'Hot lips Mendeneres – on again, off again Alexander Mendeneres – where the hell are you?'

As if in answer to her question, a knock sounded on the door. But with no time at all, it was opened, as though the person lived there. Alexander Renaldo Mendeneres stood framed in the open doorway.

'Hrummph!' Dani snorted. 'In the United

239

States, it's customary to wait until you're invited to enter.'

'But why? I'm paying the rent.'

'Oh no you're not!' At the blank look he gave her, Dani added, 'This house belongs to my brother and myself. You've contributed nothing to it.'

'Should I go outside and knock and wait?' He asked teasingly.

'Yes!' Her thoughts swung back to the litter box.

'You're being childish,' he snapped.

'Childish! Speaking of children, I wonder if you would be so eager to clean up the mess your daughter created.'

'Enough of this banter, I've more important things on my mind. Why are you complaining? I've paid you well!'

'There are some things your money can't buy, and I'm one of those things. And I'm returning your money now and I'm also returning your daughter.'

He eyed her vehemence and wondered what Maria had done to bring on this tirade. It never occurred to him that he, alone, was the object of her anger.

Alex smiled winsomely and took the laundry basket from her arm.

'Winsomeness is not your style, Mr Mendeneres. Either you have it or you don't, and you don't.'

Suddenly brisk, 'Whatever your trivial

problem is with Maria, I'm sure you'll solve it. Enough!' he barked.

Seething inwardly, Dani allowed him to take the basket from her. She plopped on to the deep, comfortable sofa and lit a cigarette as she propped her feet on the coffee table. She wiggled her big toe through the hole in her sneaker, all the while wishing she could put his head through something just as small, so she could squeeze it. 'Chauvinistic, masochistic male,' she muttered under her breath. She puffed furiously on the cigarette, blowing a steady stream in his direction.

'You smoke, too...'

'All things in moderation,' Dani chimed in with his last inevitable words. Another puff of smoke for the speaker.

'Where's Maria?'

'Next door. Where else?'

'Good, because I have to talk to you.'

'In other words, you're going to talk and I'm going to listen, is that it?' Dani smirked.

'Exactly,' he said coolly.

'Hrmmph!' Dani snorted. 'There are those who are ignorant beyond insult! Well, get on with it.'

'Now listen to me carefully, Dani, because I don't have the time to go through this twice.' He had her attention.

'My mother forwarded a letter to me from Rome. It's the letter I've been waiting for.

Generations of Mendeneres have waited for. I'm booked on the afternoon flight leaving from Kennedy Airport. I must go to Rome. I've got to explain what has happened. It can't be done through a wire or over the phone. I'm responsible for the scrolls and I must explain to Cardinal Palmerini in person.'

Dani sat mutely. 'But you can't go! You're the only deterrent against Valerie. I can't accept the responsibility any longer. What if something happens? Alex, you'll have to send Maria back to Argentina,' she ended breathlessly. Dani steeled herself against the silent pleading in his eyes.

'A bargain is a bargain, Miss Arnold,' he said imperiously. 'Somehow I never thought you would renege on a gentlemen's agreement.'

'That's it! That's it! Well, Mr Mendeneres, I'm not a gentleman, or haven't you noticed?'

'That's just a figure of speech. Now be sensible, Dani. You know I can't send Maria back to Argentina.'

'I'm being sensible. Send her back. It's too much responsibility.' Tears stung her eyes. 'I wasn't cut out for this mothering bit. I have things to do and places to go. I'm sorry, Alex. She's got to go.'

Alex panicked at the determination in Dani's voice. When he saw her tears, he softened. He knew she wasn't just being obstinate or selfish. She loved the child and was afraid something would happen to her. 'My business shouldn't take long. Two, three days at the most.'

Dani stared at him, startled by the softness in his voice.

'Believe me, there isn't another person I would entrust Maria with.'

Dani looked at the entreaty in his coal-black eyes and she felt weak. She stared at the firm set of his chiseled jaw before she dropped her gaze. She watched as his large brown hands clenched at his sides. She knew that if she persisted, Alex would relieve her of her duties to Maria. But was that what she really wanted?

'On one condition,' the smoothness of her own voice surprised her.

'Anything. Just put a name to it.'

'On your word as a Mendeneres?' she noticed his fists were now unclenched.

'Yes, on my word as a Mendeneres.' A smile tugged at the corners of his mouth.

'Good! Clean the bathroom!'

Silence hung in the air.

'Agh!' he sighed at last. 'Where's the broom?'

'Broom? You're going to need more than a broom!'

Later, Dani gazed appreciatively around the sweet smelling room. 'I couldn't have done a better job myself.' Putting the finishing touches to her make-up, she turned to face her reflection in the full-length mirror hanging on the bathroom door.

The warm tones of her dress deepened the gray of her eyes. She swept her dark hair back and tied it loosely with a soft, gray scarf. Dani admired the silver hoops in her ears, making a mental note to wear her hair like this more often. Smoothing her hands over the sleek lines of the dress, she once again thought that it was worth spending her week's salary on the outfit.

Gracefully, she shrugged into the matching jacket, picked up her soft black kid handbag and exited the bathroom.

Walking into the living-room, Maria was the first to notice her. 'Oh, Dani. You look bee-yoo-ti-full. Doesn't she, Papa?'

Alex turned to view the object of Maria's admiration. 'Yes, beautiful,' he said in his soft melodious accent, but he was not speaking to his daughter. Maria looked at her father quizzically.

Dani gazed into his unreadable eyes and flushed at the sound of his words.

'Well, I think she's gorgeous!' Maria continued to babble as Alex ushered her out the door to the car.

Alex maneuvered the Lincoln into the

parking space as if it were a toy. He handed Dani the keys and cautioned her to fill the gas tank.

The airport was a bustle of activity. Dani allowed Alex to see the smirk on her face as he took his luggage from the trunk of the car. So he had already packed to leave for Rome before he came to discuss it with me! How sure can one be? Alex attempted to explain the packed luggage but found himself suddenly flustered beneath her squelching gaze.

At the feeble attempt he made, Dani turned on her heel and dragged Maria by the arm over to the vending machine. 'Wouldn't you like a candy bar, Maria?'

Alex watched her nose rise in the air as she turned away from him. 'Women!'

The loudspeaker blared, jarring Dani's thoughts. 'Flight 312 for Rome, boarding at Gate 9 East.' The trio hurried down the long ramp to the reception room just outside the gate. Hurriedly, Alex bent over Maria and placed a resounding kiss on her cheek. As he picked up his bag to go, Maria grabbed his arm and pulled him backward, nearly knocking him off his feet.

'But you didn't kiss Dani! You're going all the way to Rome and you didn't kiss Dani!'

The other passengers turned around to look, knowing smiles on their faces. Dani flushed. 'I'll throttle you, Maria, when I get you home,' she hissed. Then louder. 'You better hurry, Alex. You're going to miss your plane.'

'But Papa,' Maria insisted as she pushed Dani forward.

'All right, Maria. Hush.' He bent over to give Dani a peck on the cheek just as a passenger jostled against her, pushing her closer to Alex. She heard his suitcase fall to the floor and all of a sudden his arms were around her, crushing her to him. His warm lips seared hers. He released her as quickly as he had embraced her. Dani looked into Alex's eyes and found no answer to her unasked question.

Valerie posed on the arm of the brocaded regency sofa, a cigarette poised at the red slash of her lips. 'Are you going to tell me, Eugene, or are you going to continue to play this little game of cat and mouse?' Her voice was controlled, only the slight shaking of her hand as it brought the cigarette to her mouth betrayed her nervousness.

'Why, Val?' Eugene asked snidely. 'I thought parlor games were right up your alley. Now stop this and tell me where the scrolls are or I'll—'

'You'll what?' came the menacing question. 'No, I think I'll keep the whereabouts of the scrolls to myself for the time being. I don't want any slip-ups.'

'What slip-ups? I don't understand you at all. If it wasn't for me, you wouldn't have the scrolls.'

'Yes, and now that I've got them, what good are they doing me? We've come to a dead end as far as selling them.'

'You know what, Val? I think the value of the scrolls is in your head. And you know what else? I think the only person dumb enough to pay anything for them is your dear husband, Alex.'

'Now look here, Eugene. Just because I couldn't make a sale with that egocentric, poor excuse of a man, that ... that...'

'Go on, say it. The word louse used to be a part of your vernacular, before you married Alex.'

'All right then, louse. But what right did you have to try and hide the scrolls from me? What right?' she screeched.

'The right of a man looking out for his, shall we say, vested interest?' Quickly, without warning, Eugene seized her slim wrist and wrenched it, causing Valerie to cry out in pain. 'How dumb do you think I am? Don't you think I can see those wheels turning in your head? If you think I'll give you a chance to trade off those scrolls for Maria, you've got another thought coming. You're sick, Val. Sick with revenge. You don't even want that kid. You're only using her to get back at Alex.' He gave her arm a final wrench, and Valerie shrieked with pain.

'I'm sick! What about you, you loath-some—?'

'Yes, sick! You're sick!' he snarled a second time. Calming himself, Eugene smiled and let loose with a disgusted snort. 'I'm not such a bad sort. I'm only a guy trying to turn a profit, but I'm not heartless. If I thought for one minute that the kid meant anything to you, I might be inclined to see it your way.'

'Stop playing the great humanitarian with me, Eugene. You forget I know you too well!'

'Yes, and I know you. You have about as much mother love as our mother had for us ... none. You'll find out where the scrolls are after I make the deal with Alex.'

Valerie moved toward the bedroom, stumbling over the small gilt edge table that stood in the center of the room. She turned and gave the table a vicious kick, jarring a mechanism in the typewriter that rested on it, causing the carriage to zip over to the far left, ringing the margin warning bell.

'And that,' she shrieked. 'Why do you keep that infernal thing in the center of the room? Most intelligent people use computers. That pornographic novel, that new D. H. Lawrence ... Bah!' She slammed her foot into the carrying-case resting beneath the table.

Eugene clutched her arm and pushed her

away from his portable typewriter. 'Cool it...'

'What's that supposed to mean? That I'm not supposed to mind it that you've taken the scrolls and you're going to cheat me?'

Eugene bent to retrieve a fallen piece of paper, his back to Valerie. 'You know, Val, I worry about you.'

Uncontrollable rage rushed through Valerie. She bent over and grasped the typewriter case by the handle. Just as Eugene was straightening himself, she brought the case into a full swing aiming for his head, striking him in the temple.

Eugene faltered, stumbling toward her, an expression of stunned surprise on his twisted, pain-racked features. Valerie calmly placed the case under the table and reached out to Eugene. 'You should know better than to mess with me, Eugene.' Before she could touch him, he crumpled into a heap on the floor before the sofa.

Fifteen

Dani switched off the late evening news and watched the small dot of light fade into oblivion. Sighing wearily, she added another log to the dying flames. As an afterthought, she threw in a handful of cones and watched the fire leap and dance. There would be no sleep for her tonight.

Wearily, she got up from her comfortable reclining position on the deep sofa and looked out of the huge bay window. She forced herself to stare – unblinking – at the swirling rain. Quickly, before she could change her mind, she threw open the huge oak door and stepped out on to the wide porch. Only the heavy aluminum awning shielded her from the lashing storm. The tall girl watched in horror as lightning withered and snaked its way across the Cimmerian darkness. The mammoth eighty-foot tulip tree in the front yard dipped and swayed crazily in the heavy wind. Shivering, she clasped her arms around her and walked back into the house. Carefully, she locked the door and slid the chain. She made her way slowly to the tidy kitchen to check the lock on the back door, and fastened it. Turning off the light and switching the small night light over the sink to 'on', she sat down in the semi-darkness.

I feel like a cat on a hot griddle, Dani thought gloomily. I wonder if all mothers feel this. 'I doubt it,' she murmured. They would hardly be in the position Alex had placed her in. A feeling of gloom settled over her like a mantle. 'God, I have to shake this feeling. I need a drink,' she said aloud to the empty kitchen.

'What you need, Dani old girl, is not one but two drinks,' she continued to talk to herself. Setting the drink on the coffee table, she walked on tiptoe into Maria's room to check the child. The small night light bathed the room in a faint, dim orange glow. Adjusting her eyes to the near darkness, she missed the wide-eyed stare of the child. Just as her own eyes sought the small form in the trundle bed, the child's eyes squeezed shut. Softly, Dani tiptoed from the room.

Maria lay in the warm softness and cuddled Bismarck to her chest. She's upset, the child thought wretchedly. Dani was always in bed by midnight. She looked at the small clock: one ten. Something was wrong. It must have something to do with her father. She stared at the ceiling, a sick

251

feeling settling in her stomach. For the first time since coming to this country, she wished she was back home in her own bed.

In the living-room, Dani added another log to the fire. She jumped backward as a shower of sparks spurted over the hearth. Like a kaleidoscope, she thought tiredly. Making still another nightcap, she deliberately added more gin than the drink called for. The hell with moderation, she thought nastily. She took a mighty gulp of the tart drink and suddenly stamped her foot. Damn, damn, damn! 'Damn Alexander Renaldo Mendeneres,' she said, throwing the drink, glass and all into the roaring flames.

Maria, standing in shocked silence in the bedroom doorway, quickly scuttled back into bed. 'She's upset with Papa,' she said to the sleeping cat. 'I thought Dani liked Papa.' Once more the child lay awake gazing at the ceiling.

Dani looked at her watch: three thirty-three. Would this night ever end? The sharp shrilling of the phone shattered the silence of the room. Dani's heart leaped at the sound. Who could be calling her at this late hour? Certainly not Stash. He never called, he just showed up unannounced. The Alperts' house was dark and Alex was in Rome. Quickly, she reached for the phone before it waked Maria. Probably some drunk.

'Hello,' Dani said softly.

'Miss Arnold, Miss Danielle Arnold? This is Valerie Mendeneres.' She made the whole statement sound like a question.

'Yes. This is Danielle Arnold.' She hoped her voice didn't sound as shocked as she felt.

'I've been trying for some hours now to reach my husband. So far I have been unsuccessful. I would like to speak to him, please.'

'What makes you think he's here? Do you have any idea what time it is?' Dani hedged as she tried to figure out the reason for the call. 'You people certainly have a lot of nerve,' she finally blustered.

'Come now, Miss Arnold. We are both women of the world. We both know why my husband would be there. I would like to speak to him, please,' she said, demanding, arrogant.

A whisper of fear skittered up Dani's spine at the tone of the other woman's voice. 'I'm sorry, but Mr Mendeneres isn't here.'

'I have no choice but to believe you at the moment,' Valerie continued. 'You will please give him this message—'

'I am afraid, Mrs Mendeneres,' Dani interrupted suddenly, 'that you will have to give him your own message. I don't expect to see your husband, today or in the next few days. What in the world makes you think I am your husband's keeper? Call Federal Express if you want to send a message.'

'Your very actions, my dear.' The cold, dismissive voice turned deadly sounding. The whisper of fear skittering up and down Dani's spine was now a full-blown shout.

'What actions?' Dani blurted. The malevolent Valerie ignored her question.

'Tell Alexander that I will meet him at four thirty at the information booth in Penn Station. Tomorrow! You will also tell him that I will wait exactly ten minutes. If he is not there, the deal is off.'

'Wait, wait, I can't reach Mr Mendeneres.' Dani blinked when she realized she was speaking to an empty, lifeless phone line. It was dead. Just as dead as she felt.

Dani stood with the receiver gripped in her hand, eyes staring blankly. What deal was Valerie talking about? Alex never said he'd made a deal with his wife. Her skull felt as though it were splitting in two. 'It's too much!' she moaned. 'Too much!'

Once again, she failed to see the small, still form in the bedroom doorway.

Maria crept slowly back to bed. She shifted the weighty cat to a more comfortable position. 'That was my mother,' she whispered. 'First my father angers Dani, now my mother does the same thing. Soon Dani will hate me, too.' The child longed to rush into the living-room to hug the tall, strange girl who had made her so happy. Somehow, she knew that Dani would not have wanted that. Then she questioned the sleeping cat. 'How will she know that I love her with all my heart, even if my father and mother don't.' She glanced at the small bedside clock: four forty. She buried her head in Bismarck's fur and wept uncontrollably.

Suddenly, Bismarck struggled free of the child's grasp and arched his back. Jumping from the bed, he stalked to the dark corner of the bedroom. Fur on end, he began spitting and snarling.

Maria moved to the foot of the bed and peered into the dim shadows. 'It's Brother Gian, Bismarck. Do not be afraid. He is here to watch me. Now everything will be all right,' she whispered. 'Come here, Bismarck,' she called softly. The huge tom, at the sound of the child's voice, relaxed and hopped back on to the bed. The child knew she would have to leave in the morning before her beloved Dani came to hate her. Now that the Monk was here everything would be all right. Wherever she went, the Monk would follow. With the heavy decision made, her choking sobs diminished and she slept.

Dani cradled the phone and brought her eyes back into focus. Now what was she to do? Damn the man. Every damn time she needed him, he was off somewhere. 'I don't have an address or even a phone number in Rome where I can reach him,' she wailed silently. A picture of her trying to get through to the Vatican flashed before her. Suddenly, she giggled and the tension she had felt all night long was gone. It was simply a question of logistics. Quickly, she poured herself a cup of coffee. She lit a cigarette and let her mind race. Dani sat quietly, rejecting and accepting. Finally satisfied, she heaved a weary yawn and decided to call it a night or what was left of the night. Dani looked at the small square watch on her slim wrist: five fifty-eight. The dawn of a new day.

Maria crept from the warm bed and pushed Bismarck on to the floor. She tiptoed to Dani's door and looked in. Dani lay fully dressed across the bed, deep in sleep. Quietly, she closed the door. Opening a small can of cat food, she slopped it haphazardly into the dish. She poured herself a small glass of juice and reached for a box of cereal. Turning on the television, she sat munching the sweet-flavored tidbits. She would leave around eleven after she borrowed Kelly's bicycle. Setting the cereal aside, she counted her small hoard of money. Forty-seven dollars and ninety-six cents. That would hold her till she got to the city and wired her grandmother to send her a plane ticket. The object was to take nothing with her except her money. Maria continued to munch and chew thoughtfully as she watched *Felix the Cat* scamper across the wide screen.

As was her custom after breakfast, Maria made her bed and changed the litter box. She brushed her teeth and dressed. Back in the kitchen, she cleaned up the spilled cat food. She had just washed her hands when there was a knock on the back door. Carefully, she peered around the colorful curtains. 'Stash,' she almost squealed. Maria removed the chain and opened the door. The red-bearded giant gave her a quick hug and whirled her in the air. 'How's my favorite *noodge*?' Not waiting for a reply, he continued, 'Guess what? I came to take you and Dani to the circus. So where's the warden? Go get her!'

Maria's face fell. 'I'm sorry, Stash, but Dani is sleeping and she told me not to wake her. She did not get to bed at all last night. She said it was some kind of virus and that I should be quiet and let her sleep all day. Perhaps you could take me to the circus. Just the two of us. I am sure Dani wouldn't mind.'

'Why not?' Stash shrugged. 'Get your coat and I'll write Dani a note. We should be back sometime after dinner. This way she'll have the whole day to herself.'

Carefully, he penciled the note.

Dear Dani,

Arrived bright eyed and bushy-tailed this morning at nine to invite you and Maria to the circus. She told me you have a virus. Some luck. I only catch colds. Viruses always sound so important. I'll have Maria back after dinner. Sorry I missed you.

Take care.

Stash

Stash placed the note on the round wooden table next to the empty cat food tin. He picked the tin up and threw it in the trash bag. Several moist balls of food dropped from the rim. He looked for a cloth to wipe up the spill. Seeing none, he shrugged. Maria came into the kitchen, eyed the note and grimaced. Quickly, they left the small house and headed for New York.

Sometime shortly after the noon hour, Bismarck, tired of being on his own, strutted nonchalantly into the kitchen. He looked around in total disdain. He eyed the empty dish that bore his name and sniffed at the trashcan. Once more he looked around, sniffed again. Leaping on to the chair, he let his eyes move over the tabletop. Pouncing on the minuscule balls of cat food, he licked his whiskers then padded over the shiny surface of the tabletop knocking the small piece of paper to the floor. Jumping from the table, he caught the paper as it landed. He clawed at it and heard the crisp crackle as his two front paws crunched the paper into a ball. Obsessively, he played with the small scrap for over an hour. He eyed the shreds of now limp paper and lay down under the table.

Hours later, Dani climbed wearily from her bed. Glancing at the small bedside clock over her shoulder, she was shocked at the time: one forty-five. She walked through the old house and could find no trace of Maria. Bismarck was asleep under the kitchen table. She checked the litter box. Clean. She looked into the shallow red dish that belonged to him and saw a faint trace of dry food. Maria had taken care of him. Why wasn't he with her?

The chain and latch were off the back door. The front door was still locked. Dani walked out the back door and called the child. Stillness hung like a pall. Then she remembered. The new school opened today. All the kids would be gone. So would Mrs Alpert, as she taught the fifth grade. She called again. Bismarck stirred and joined Dani on the back porch. He looked at her reproachfully. 'Well, where is she?' Dani demanded. For an answer, Bismarck re-traced his steps to the kitchen and lay down under the table.

The first faint fingers of panic gripped Dani's stomach. Back in her bedroom, she changed her rumpled clothes hurriedly and threw on a heavy jacket. This time she unlatched the front door and went out to the winding, curved road. Kelly's bike was propped against the holly tree in his front yard. Wherever Maria had wandered off to, she had evidently walked. Next, she headed for the worn path by the brook that led to the woods. Dani was halfway up the path when she suddenly knew, she couldn't explain why, that Maria wasn't in the woods.

Still she called feebly, knowing full well that there would be no reply. Her stomach in a knot, she headed back to the house. She had to do something. Maria wouldn't just wander off. Quite the contrary. With the boys now in school, she would be lost and stick close to home. Something had happened to her! If the front door still had the chain on and the chain was off the back door, it could only mean that the little girl had opened the door to someone. Someone she must have known. Dani had warned her, repeatedly, never to open the door to anyone she didn't know. Her head started to throb. What to do? Call the police? No. If she did, Alex would have a fit.

The child would never run away, Dani was sure of that. Could Valerie have taken her? Was that why the door stood open? She had to believe that Valerie had her for the moment and that for the moment she was safe. Was that what Valerie meant last night when she called? She glanced at the kitchen clock and raced into the bathroom. Hurriedly, she applied some sketchy make-up. Brushing her hair she drew it back and tied it with a scarf. She grabbed her purse and checked the money it held. Suddenly she had a thought. Dani raced to Maria's room. Carefully, she searched for some clue. The minuscule search took ten minutes. When she finished, she was sure of only one thing. Maria's heavy jacket and her small hoard of 'mad' money were gone. Dani was more puzzled than ever. If Maria took the money, she must have had a reason. The youngster had been saving it to buy presents for her grandmother and her friends.

Wearily, Dani gave up on the wild ideas that were swirling and twirling inside her head. She looked again at the clock. She would have to hurry if she intended to take Alex's place at Penn Station. The only hope that sustained her was that she could bluff her way out of the situation. God, I'm no good at this kind of intrigue. I'm just a plain old, every-day citizen who minds her own business.

Dani picked up her camel's hair coat and car keys and left the small house, but first she left a note for the child, propped up on the mantle. 'I hope you return to read it, Maria,' she sighed.

In the driveway, Dani looked at Alex's sleek Lincoln Continental and at the four-wheel drive jeep. Without hesitating, she jumped into the colorful jeep and backed out of the driveway. Maneuvering the Lincoln was like driving a Mack truck.

For the entire journey to the city, Dani drove with her teeth clenched so hard that her jaw ached. By the Grace of God, she found a parking spot and walked the few short blocks to the train station. Once inside, she let her eyes scan the walls till she found a clock. She verified the time with the tiny watch on her wrist. It was two minutes off. She had half an hour to kill till it was time to meet Valerie. Spotting a phone booth, she fished about in her change purse for a dime. Dialing Stash's private number, Dani counted... Seven, eight, nine... 'Hello?'

'This is Dani Arnold. Can I speak to Stash, please?'

'Hi, Dani. This is Brad. Sorry, but Stash isn't here today. I'm in charge.'

Dani felt limp. She had been counting on Stash to be there. She needed somebody to talk to. 'Do you know where he is, Brad? It's important.'

'No idea, Dani. He gave me the word yesterday. All he said was that he had a heavy date today with not one but two girls. Sorry I can't be of more help. Is there anything I can do?'

'No. Thanks anyway, Brad.' Slowly Dani hung up the phone. She was really counting on Stash. Until now he'd always been there for her. Her eyes smarted, she had always been able to count on Stash. Double damn.

Dani headed back to the main concourse and eyed the milling people. There wasn't a soul she recognized. Moving over to an unoccupied bench, she sat down. She had a clear, unobstructed view of the information booth. Now all she had to do was wait. And wait she did.

Dani clenched and unclenched her fists, getting up intermittently to stretch her legs. She looked at her watch for what must have been the hundredth time. It was ten minutes of six. Where was Valerie? Dani sat back down and continued to stare at the throngs of people bent on catching their commuter trains. Her shoulders slumped in defeat. There was no point in waiting any longer. She might as well leave. She knew Alex would never forgive her but there was nothing else for her to do. Dejectedly, she rose to her feet.

Never in her life had she felt so helpless, so afraid for another human being. What was she to do? Where to turn? 'If there was only something I could do,' she murmured softly. Sitting and waiting was unbearable. I have to do something, anything, she thought. I'll comb this station from one corner to the next, she thought viciously. I'll find her if it's the last thing I do.

Sixteen

'Dani!' She heard her name being called. She swiveled around.

'Christ, am I glad to see you.' It was Stash. Dani had never seen him in such an agitated state before. He was blithering like an idiot.

'What are you mumbling about?'

Stash told his story. 'So you see, when the kid said you were sick, I thought I was doing you a favor by taking her off your hands for the day. Say, you don't look very sick to me,' he said suspiciously.

'That's because I'm not sick. I have no idea why Maria would tell you a thing like that. You might have left me a note for God's sake. I was worried sick. Where is she?'

'I did leave you a note and I don't know where she is. She's gone, she flew the coop.'

'What do you mean she's gone? Why didn't you watch her? I feel sorry for the woman you marry,' Dani said nastily. 'How did you lose her? How could you?' she wailed.

'Well, I guess it was inevitable. After four bottles of Pepsi Cola and three hot dogs and two cotton candies, she said she had to go the bathroom. I offered to take her and she gave me such a look that I didn't offer a second time. I didn't start to worry till she was gone for half an hour. Then I asked the people who were standing next to me to watch out for her while I went off to search. After all, Dani, she is ten years old and she can read the his and her signs,' he said defensively in response to his friend's severe look.

Dani nodded wearily. 'I know it's not your fault. Just tell me one thing. Do you remember the time? Was it around four fifteen or four thirty?'

'Yeah. How did you know? It was almost over and I figured I better let her go, so we could beat the rush getting out. Christ, I'm sorry Dani. I've been combing this damn station ever since. In fact, I was just about to get the police when I spotted you.'

'Come here, Stash,' Dani said, directing him to the bench she had just vacated. 'I guess it was to be expected. Valerie waiting downstairs by the information booth, Maria upstairs in Madison Square Garden. I can just see Maria looking over the railing at the same time Valerie is gazing around. Maria wouldn't have been expecting her mother, but Valerie would be quick as a fox. The rest is simple,' Dani sighed.

'Jesus, I really screwed it up for you, didn't

I?' Stash said remorsefully.

Dani nodded wearily.

'Do you know where the kid's mother lives?'

'No. How could I know?'

'Well think. Maybe her husband said something, or the kid. I mean, after all, if it were my ex-wife, I'd probably tell everyone where she was in the hopes she would re-marry and let me off the hook.'

'Oh, Stash, be sensible. The Mendeneres aren't like that.'

'Well, what *are* they like? Maybe we can get some kind of clue as to where she hangs her hat.'

Dani recounted everything she could re-member. 'We're right back where we started. I have no clue, Stash,' she sighed.

'You're right. The only thing left is to start calling all the big hotels and see if she's registered. Sounds like she would only go first class and there aren't that many big hotels left in the city any more. Come on,' he said, grabbing her by the arm and heading for the nearest phone booth.

They pooled their quarters. Dani looked up a number and dialed. Twenty minutes later, they struck pay dirt. 'Aha! She's regis-tered at the Plaza.'

Stash looked at Dani. 'Do you want to call her or go unannounced? Just name it, I'm right behind you.'

267

'We'll go there,' Dani said, her heart taking on an extra beat. 'I left the jeep in the parking lot a couple of blocks away.'

'We'll take a cab. It's faster.'

'Wait a minute, Stash,' Dani said, laying a soft hand on his muscular arm. 'This is something I have to do alone. I know you'll understand.' She spoke quickly, stalling any comment Stash might be on the verge of making. Her eyes pleaded with the bearded giant to see her point.

Stash looked into the murky, gray eyes and nodded. 'Gotcha,' he grinned. 'But,' he said shaking a large ham-like fist, 'if you have any inkling that there may be trouble, send up an alarm. I'm going back to the club. You can reach me there.'

Dani nodded gratefully, tears in her eyes. She knew that Stash was chomping at the bit. It was just like him to give her her head and be around to pick up the pieces. Quickly, she kissed the bearded cheek and left without a backward glance. She walked blindly to the 34th Street exit and hailed the first cab she saw. 'The Plaza Hotel,' she said, choking on her words. 'Yes, ma'am,' the driver said in an exaggerated, polite tone.

There was no sense crying over spilled milk. She would have to do the best she could – on her own. Just as she'd been doing for a long, long time, she thought bitterly. I wonder what it would be like to have someone wait on you hand and foot, make all your decisions for you, to coddle you and care for you, she mused to herself. She gave herself a mental shake and reached for her wallet as the cab glided to a stop in front of the hotel. She told the driver to keep the change and got a very large wink and an overly polite 'thank you'. Dani grinned at the expression on the cabbie's face. He probably thinks I live here, she grimaced.

Dani walked over to the desk and inquired about Valerie.

'Room six thirteen,' the clerk said politely, as he picked up the house phone to announce her.

Seeing his intention, Dani smiled winningly. 'Don't bother to announce me. My sister is expecting me.'

The clerk, only happy to oblige, smiled in return.

Nonchalantly, Dani strolled to the bank of elevators to the left of the spacious lobby and carefully pressed the 'up' button. Nervously, she resisted the impulse to look over her shoulder.

The elevator arrived and Dani took a deep breath as she stepped into the small cubicle. 'Six, please,' she said softly. Fortunately for her frame of mind, she and the elevator operator were the only occupants of the car.

The elevator slid smoothly to a stop. Mustering all the courage she possessed,

Dani marched out of the elevator and down the hall as though she knew just where she was going. She spotted room six thirteen halfway down the corridor. She stood quietly and listened. There was no sound. Quickly, she knocked. There was no answer. She knocked a second time. I knew she wouldn't come back here, Dani thought wildly. Why did I bother to come?

Once more, she knocked and waited. As if her hand had a will of its own, she grasped the doorknob and turned. The door opened without a sound. Strange, she mused to herself. No one leaves their doors open. Well, this one was, she might as well go in. The worst that could happen would be a charge of breaking and entering!

'Mrs Mendeneres,' Dani called to the empty room. Stepping inside, she closed the door softly. It was a spacious suite of rooms. The very silence thundered in her ears. Dani called again, inching her way into the dim room. Nervously, she let her gaze travel the length and width of the room. Suddenly, she stumbled as she moved in front of a pale gold, brocaded sofa. Looking down, she gasped at the wide pool of blood that had already started to turn brown at the edges. It was the man from the airport! The one that had been arguing with Valerie Mendeneres.

Taking a deep breath, Dani bent to her

knees and felt for a pulse. She knew before she touched the body that there wouldn't be one. 'Oh my God,' she backed away. 'He's dead.'

Shocked, she collided into the small, ornate desk standing in the middle of the floor. At least, in Dani's muddled state, it appeared to be in the middle of the floor. The trembling girl all but fell into the small gilt chair. Taking a deep breath, she willed her mind out of its chaotic state. She had to think. That's it, think! 'He's dead. You can't help him. Maria isn't here. Go on from here, Dani,' she told herself. Lock the door.

Stiffly, she got up from the decorative chair and raced to the door. She threw the bolt and sobbed to herself. Now you've locked yourself into a room with a dead man. 'Oh my God,' she wailed. Don't think, Dani. Move. Look all around. Maybe Valerie left some clue. Suddenly it hit her. If this was Valerie's room, what was that man doing here? And why was he dead? It was apparent that he didn't die by his own hand. That must mean that Valerie, since this was her suite ... She couldn't have! Not Maria's mother. Not Alex's wife.

'Where are you, Alex?' she moaned. 'I need you. What should I do? Should I call the police like the good citizen I am?' And then what, Dani? She could just hear them and the inquisition they would put her

271

through. Her job would go down the drain. She would become a household name. They would grill her, fingerprint her. Alex would be snuffed. And what of the child and her mother? It was just possible that Valerie knew nothing about the body. Maybe it was a burglar. She had to leave everything as it was. She had to leave the apartment and hope that somehow she wasn't connected with the man. Who in their right mind would believe the incredible story she would have to tell? Oh what tangled webs we weave, she thought wryly.

Carefully, averting her eyes from the still form, she tiptoed daintily around the spacious suite. Dani opened drawers and closets. Nothing appeared to be hidden. Valerie certainly wouldn't leave the scrolls laying around for a chance maid to spot. 'I have to be sure,' she said aloud to the empty room.

Once more, she sat down on the small gilt chair. She took a cigarette from her purse and lit it with trembling hands. Dani dropped the match into a shining crystal ashtray. Evidently, Valerie didn't smoke. But the man did, whoever he was. His fingers were yellow with nicotine stains. She had noticed that when she'd taken his pulse. I wonder how long he's been dead, she asked herself morbidly as she let her finger peck on the typewriter on the desk.

'I really don't want to know how long he's been dead,' she said to herself. 'Yes, you do,' she answered. Now get up and go over and feel his skin. You'll get some kind of an idea. That way you'll know whether or not it's possible that Valerie is involved.

Dani grasped the edges of the desk and stared at the small, cheap portable type-writer. Somehow it didn't look like anything Valerie Mendeneres would own, and she probably doesn't even know how to type.

Idly, Dani leafed through the sheaf of papers. It looked like someone was writing a pornographic novel. Dani felt herself flush as her eyes raked the pages on the top of the pile. It must belong to the man on the floor. He looked like the type that would write erotic fiction. 'To each his own,' Dani sighed as she got to her feet. Slowly, she walked to the sofa. She looked at the grayish pallor of the man's skin. He's been dead for a while, she thought.

Forcing herself to her knees, she rum-maged through his pockets. Keys, cigar-ettes, matches. Nothing relevant. Dani gave a mighty heave and rolled the body on its side. The lifeless form emitted a low, gur-gling groan. Petrified, Dani jumped to her feet and backed away, stumbling against the sofa. Her heart pounded rapidly, beating its tattoo heavily against her constricted chest. She raised a quivering hand to brush away a stray lock of her hair. Unable to contain herself any longer and suddenly realizing what had happened, she gave way to a tearful, trembling laugh which threatened to build to mounting hysteria. Enough murder plots had passed her desk for her to realize that air trapped in the body's lungs would escape if a corpse were to be moved.

Dani took a deep breath and willed herself to be astute and analytical.

He's been dead three or four hours, she judged uneasily.

The time element was right. Valerie could have done it before she left for the train station. Somehow, she couldn't picture her coming back and whacking the guy over the head with Maria in attendance. And he wasn't an intruder. Not if the typewriter and the manuscript pages were his. There had also been evidence of another occupant – in the bathroom, there were two toothbrushes and a set of military brushes.

No, she decided, he had to be staying with Valerie, which would explain the typewriter.

The hell with it. Dani looked around to be sure she left nothing of hers in sight. Carefully she picked up the stub of her cigarette and dropped it in her coat pocket. She looked at her hands encased in the black kid gloves and thanked God she had had the sense to wear them.

I have to go home, she thought wildly. My

God, what if Stash had been here? He would have called the police without a second thought. If there was one thing you could say about Stash, it was that he was civic minded. Dani giggled hysterically as she once more let her gaze scan the room. Satisfied, she opened the door and peered out into the corridor. Empty. She picked up the 'do not disturb' sign from the small table and hung it on the door. This way an over-ambitious maid wouldn't come pussy-footing into the room and drop dead of a heart attack.

She reset the latch and scurried down the hallway to the elevator. God, I hope that desk clerk has bad eyes, Dani thought suddenly. Too late now. And the elevator operator, would he remember? Possibly. She would take the stairs.

Opening the side door of the spacious lobby, her eyes immediately sought for and found the nasally desk clerk. His back to her, he was having an earnest conversation with one of the bellboys. He didn't appear to notice her. Swiftly, Dani left the elevator, walking across the immense lobby and out into the dark night. She walked away quickly from the huge hotel and hailed a cab as soon she was out of sight. The doorman might remember her. Her mind whirled.

Dani directed the taxi to where she had left the jeep and leaned back exhausted

275

against the rough leather of the seat.

Suddenly, a phrase her mother used to say popped into her mind. God's in his heaven and all's right with the world. Everything was not all right with the world. She had committed some kind of crime by not calling the police. Had she now become an accomplice? If she were caught, would she be put in jail? She had heard about the Tombs, did they put women there? Would Alex be able to get her out? Would Stash turn against her? For a moment, she felt terribly upset that Stash's opinion of her would change. Good, old, 'straight arrow' Stash. He never compromised his ideals. There should be more people like him in the world, Dani thought sadly.

Dani paid the driver, giving him a healthy tip. Once she had stepped into the waiting jeep, she turned the key and started the engine. She pulled into the steady stream of early evening traffic. Her eyes on the other steadily moving cars, she fumbled for a knob and turned up the radio full blast to drown out her thoughts. As she swerved off the highway on to Route 31, the tension that had gripped her began to ease. Now she was in her home territory. Feeling safer than she had in hours, Dani listened with half an ear to Frank Sinatra as he sang about strangers in the night. Hell, she had been a stranger since this whole mess started. 'Dooby dooby

276

do,' she mimicked the singer.

Snapping off the radio, she turned the wheel and swung into Hollow Road. Five more minutes and she would be home. She parked the jeep under a tulip tree and climbed out, with the weight of the world on her shoulders.

Wearily, the tired girl climbed the worn fieldstone steps to the front porch. She checked the mailbox. No mail. She entered the dark house.

The note to Maria was still on the mantle. She eyed the squat, black phone. It almost looked obscene in its silence. Dani willed it to ring. It remained silent. Having tossed her bag and coat on the chair, she made herself a drink. On second thought, she needed a fire to calm her. Dani threw some small logs into the fireplace, wadded up yesterday's paper and struck a match.

Once she had kicked off her shoes, she leaned back, drink in hand, into the softness of the old sofa.

Dani watched the bright orange flames flicker and dance as she sipped her tart drink. Noticing the glass was nearly empty, she refilled it and, again, became absorbed by the wavering flames, letting her mind have its way as she relived the entire afternoon. If she could change things ... She wasn't sure she would have done anything differently.

Suddenly, Bismarck jumped on her lap. 'Hi, old buddy,' Dani crooned softly to the huge cat. 'Did you miss me? Bet you're hungry. Come on. I'll feed you.' It dawned on her as she got to her feet and swayed dizzily that she hadn't eaten all day. 'Let's face it, Bismarck, you can't drink on an empty stomach. Let's see what we have here. Left-over macaroni and cheese. That's good enough for you. You need more variety in your diet anyway.' She spooned out the congealed glob into his dish and smirked to herself as she watched the finicky cat turn up his nose and walk away reproachfully.

'Hmm. Things are tough all over, cat. If you're hungry enough, you'll eat it,' Dani rummaged some more and fished out a wrinkled apple and two slices of pre-wrapped cheese that were dry around the edges. Quickly, she ate both and downed a glass of milk in two swallows.

Once again, she seated herself comfortably before the fire. Something wasn't gelling. What was it? Carefully, step by step, she let her mind go back over her recent activities. There was something wrong, she knew it, but she couldn't quite place her finger on it. Then she went over her movements in the hotel suite. Whatever it was, it refused to surface. Dani flushed again as she recalled the phraseology of the pornographic novel.

'That's it!' she shouted to the empty room. 'That's it!' Those pages were nothing but smut. There didn't appear to be any story-line to what she had glanced through. She wasn't a junior editor for nothing. Hadn't she almost finished a cookbook? Besides, when she wrote, she smoked incessantly. She would light up, place the cigarette in the ashtray and let it burn out. The dead man's hands had been heavily stained with nicotine. The papers appeared to be freshly typed, yet the ashtrays were sparkling clean. It didn't add up. Unless it was all a decoy. Mentally, she pictured the size and weight of the small, portable typewriter. Not only that, but most people wouldn't even bother to remove the typewriter from its case when it was so small. That was one of the advantages of a portable. Not to have to lift it in and out of its case. The case – where was it? Why not a laptop instead of an old-fashioned typewriter? It was under the small, spindly desk. She remembered kick-ing it with her foot. The desk! It was a woman's desk, just a wobbly little table, actually. That's it! Somehow she couldn't picture the elegant Valerie bothering to write porno garbage. Was one or the other trying to outmaneuver the other? Probably so. It made sense.

Now what do I do? You know what you have to do, Dani. 'Oh no,' she groaned aloud. 'I could never go back in there. Besides, I locked the door. Locks can be picked,' her other self answered. 'But he's dead, I couldn't look at him again. You can do whatever you have to do, Dani. You just have to understand how important it is to you. It's for Maria and Alex. What if someone sees me? Wear a disguise,' the daring, quick-thinking Dani answered.

'Hmfph!' she snorted.

'I don't have the guts,' she wailed.

'Why argue? I'm going to do it.'

Dani scrubbed her face bare of make-up. Within minutes, her appearance was altered sharply. She penciled in a high-arched brow, added a line at the outer corners of her eyes, giving her a slight oriental look. She added more color than usual to her high cheekbones and rubbed in a darker make-up around her nose and chin. As a disguise, her efforts left a lot to be desired.

Having pulled her hair back into a skin-tight chignon, she added a floppy hat. Dani squinted at her reflection. It would have to do. Rummaging in the closet, she withdrew a black maxi-coat. She would take Alex's Lincoln and hope for the best.

Back in the living-room, she looked at the phone, wishing it would ring. Dani settled the screen around the fireplace and checked the ashtrays. She turned off the lamp and switched on a small night-light. Carefully, she locked the door behind her.

Unknown to Dani, by the time she had the door of the Lincoln open, the phone inside had started – and stopped – ringing. And the overseas operator had said her apologies to the American on the other end of the phone.

An hour later, Dani successfully found a parking place. *My lucky day. I find a space not once but twice and then I find a dead body.*

Walking sedately up to the hotel entrance, she clenched and unclenched her hands a dozen times. There was a different doorman. Luck was on her side. Dani squared her shoulders and stepped regally through the door. Looking neither to the left nor the right, she headed straight for the elevator and was once again in luck.

Women spilled from the elevator, laughing happily over something that must have transpired within the car. 'Five,' she said in a husky voice. The young operator stood staring straight ahead, engrossed in his own thoughts. Dani left the car and immediately looked for directions to the stairway.

Satisfied, she walked briskly through the door and walked up one flight. A violent chill washed over her as she approached room six thirteen. Cautiously, she knocked and stood back to wait, knowing there would be no answer. Her 'do not disturb' sign was still intact. Scanning the hallway, she withdrew a credit card from her pocket. Just like the movies, she grimaced.

She maneuvered the small card up and down. Nuts! It always worked in the movies. She tried again and was rewarded with the sound of a tiny click. Looking over her shoulder, down the dim hallway, she heaved a sigh and entered the dark suite. Her skin crawled.

God! Where was the light? Dani fumbled as she tried to remember, to the left of the door. Her hand struggled with the switch plate. Feeling the small protrusion, she snapped the overhead foyer light to 'on'. The room was bathed in a faint, rosy glow. Dani snapped the lock once more and leaned against the door for support. I wonder how cat burglars do it? She shuddered.

She pulled on her black kid gloves as she advanced into the room. She saw that it was the same as she had left it, four hours ago.

Investigating the area under the tiny table, she saw the beat-up metal case of the portable. With long strides, she had it in her hand. Heart fluttering madly, she hardly dared to press the clasp. With shaking hands, she managed to open it. She drew in her breath and let loose a very articulate 'oh'. So, she had been right. There, nestled in layers of silk, were rolls of parchment.

Quickly, she snapped the case and raced to Valerie's room. Dani looked in the closet for a small weekend bag. She withdrew a handsome black, alligator carry-on and, before she could change her mind, stuffed the typewriter case inside. The bag closed, she let her gaze rake the room. Satisfied, she turned off the light.

Averting her gaze from the lifeless form on the carpet, she stood once more by the small gilt table. She lifted each page of paper. Nothing. Just pages of drivel that only a sick mind could comprehend. The camouflage had been confirmed.

Once again, she turned out all the lights and opened the door and peered down the hallway. Dani glanced at her watch. Almost one in the morning. After locking the door for the second time, she headed for the next exit sign over the stairway. She walked down all six flights and stopped, winded for the moment. Carefully and quickly, she inched the door open and looked through the narrow slit. The lobby was almost deserted. Bad luck. The same desk clerk was still on duty. Not only was he on duty, he appeared to be wide awake and extremely alert.

Dani wondered how many guests left the hotel at one in the morning carrying a suitcase. Maybe he'll think I'm trying to leave without paying the bill. I wasn't cut out for this cloak-and-dagger jazz, she moaned to herself. I'll just have to wait till he leaves his post, she thought. Sooner or later he'll have to go to the bathroom.

Sure enough, two hours and twenty minutes later, the man sauntered to the room adjacent to the desk. In a flash, Dani was through the entrance. Muttering to herself about middle-of-the-night plane departures, she whizzed past the startled doorman.

Inside the Lincoln, with the doors locked, she sat trembling. 'God's in his heaven and all's right with the world. Mama, how right you were.'

The car in gear, she drove home with myriad emotions. Tomorrow was another day. No, actually it was today. Now all she would have to do was sit and wait. Not only did she have flower power, she had barter power. And barter she would ... for Maria.

Seventeen

Valerie Mendeneres ground her teeth as she listened to Maria's sleepy sobs.

She cast a disparaging look around the dingy hotel room. Dull, drab, brown. Lit by a single naked light bulb.

Fear tightened the muscles in her stomach as she forced back the bile that rose in her throat.

'How could I have been stupid enough to let Eugene get his sticky fingers on the scrolls?' It was his own fault, it really was his own fault, she thought angrily. 'He should have told me where they were,' she defended herself. 'But oh God, I didn't mean to kill him. I didn't. I really didn't.'

Tears of self-pity ran in hot rivulets down her cheeks, smearing the artfully applied make-up. Her face was a swollen blur that mirrored her dejection. 'What am I going to do? What am I going to do?' she moaned. 'Now I have nothing left. There's nothing left.'

Suddenly, she heard Maria sob again. She cast the sleeping child a churlish look, annoyed to be interrupted by this moment of pained emotion. Valerie waited a moment longer to see if the child would stir. She did not. Once more she returned to her tortured cries of self-pity.

'I have nothing left. There's nothing left. No money. My clothes and jewelry left behind with Eugene. No scrolls. No husband. No nothing.' At the remembrance of her husband, a hopeful gleam came into her eyes. Alex will tell them for me. Alex will tell them how Eugene threatened me, used me, even threatened my child. She practised a curiously loving glance in Maria's direction. 'After all, a mother has every right to protect her child, doesn't she?'

'Ah!' she squealed. 'I forgot. Diplomatic immunity. I must have it. Oh, I'm sure I have it. If I don't, Alex will get it for me. He wouldn't let the mother of his child go to prison, would he?'

Her hopes died with the realization that Alex loved truth and righteousness. 'No, I have nothing,' she acceded. 'Nothing.'

Valerie watched the sleeping child roll over on the narrow cot that served as a bed. 'Or have I?'

Dani plugged in the electric percolator and grimaced, 'It's going to be a long night.'

She splashed cold water on her face and patted some astringent lotion sparingly.

Brushing her hair, she counted each stroke. 'I want to be wide awake when the phone rings.'

Her thoughts were with the child. Sending out messages of strength, of courage, she said to herself, 'Hang in there, Maria. Only a little while longer.'

The tiny red light glowed in the semi-darkness of the kitchen. She grabbed the pot, a cup and an ashtray, along with her cigarettes. And stationed herself by the silent phone.

The hours till dawn crawled on tortoise legs. Dani glanced at her watch for the *umteenth* time and drained the last of the coffee. It was eight ten in the morning. Mentally, she tried to calculate the time difference between New York and Rome. She shrugged. 'You're on your own from here on in, Danielle. It's time you realized that.' Her head slumped to her chest just as the phone rang, ominously. Dani restrained herself from catching it the first time. Her heart thumping, she managed to whisper 'Hello' in a controlled voice.

'Miss Arnold, this is Mrs Mendeneres.'

Dani caught the usage of the word 'Mrs', recalling the previous call when she announced herself merely as 'Valerie Mendeneres'. Remembering Eugene's cold, stiff dead body, Dani could understand Valerie's plea for the protection she may receive as

Alex's wife.

'Is my husband there?'

'No, he isn't. I told you that when you called before.' Dani's ears strained to hear background noises, yearning for some sign of Maria's presence. There was nothing.

'I'm not playing games any more, Miss Arnold. I have something Alex wants.'

'And I, Mrs Mendeneres, have something you want,' Dani said meaningfully.

'I have no idea what that could be, Miss Arnold.'

'I think we both know what I mean,' Dani replied curtly. 'Simply put, Mrs Mendeneres, the scrolls.'

'That's impossible, Eug—'

'Not as impossible as you may think. I visited your hotel yesterday afternoon. And Mrs Mendeneres, you won't believe this but there was a dead body lying in the middle of your sitting-room floor.'

'How and where did you find the scrolls?' Valerie asked, ignoring the mention of Eugene's dead body.

'Those are your words, not mine.'

'I want to talk to Alex about this. I refuse to negotiate with you.'

'You have no choice. The way I see it, you need money to help you get out of your ... difficulties. Alex will never pay money for his daughter. And I doubt, in your flight from justice, you want to be burdened with a ten-year-old child.'

Valerie, sensing the logic behind the girl's words, knew it was true. Her recourse would be to sell Alex the scrolls, but first she had to find them. Did the girl have the scrolls? If not, what was she talking about? What did she have? Valerie's mind whirled. Apparently, this woman knew about Eugene. Could she have found the scrolls by the sheerest accident? She herself had no idea where Eugene had hidden them and there was no way now that Eugene could help her. The girl was right about one thing, the child would slow her down. What to do? Bluff her way out as she always did. She would tie a rope around Maria's neck if she had to. Suddenly, as if struck by a bolt of lightning, she knew in her gut that the girl would deal.

Dani waited impatiently for the answer. Fear coursed through her body. She held her breath.

'Fine! Top of the Empire State Building at two this afternoon. I'll have Maria with me. Come alone.'

Click...

Sick with apprehension, Dani slumped wearily on to the sofa. 'Did I do right? Oh God, help me, did I do right?' Her eyes traveled to the typewriter case resting at her feet. From what Alex said, the scrolls held the hope of the world. Life for humanity, not just one small, frightened little girl. 'But I don't love humanity, I love Maria and Alex,' she whispered to the empty room. 'I have to do it.'

Dani squinted against the slanting rays of the cold November sun that had woken her. Bismarck was nudging her hopefully, yowling for his dinner – or was it lunch? She lay for a moment, confused and drained from her recent activities. Wearily, she got to her feet. 'All right, Bismarck, I'll feed you.' Secretly sad for the big, old tom, who she knew sorely missed Maria, she cooed, 'I miss her, too, but she'll be back. Now I have to get milk.'

Walking to the door, she noticed an oblong of yellow paper that had been slipped through the mail slot. Quickly, she reached for it and slit the envelope. It was a cable from Alex:

'Arriving Kennedy Airport two forty-five, Thursday. Flight 23, Al Italia.'

Dani groaned. 'You ... you...' Words failed her. Bismarck wailed again at this second delay.

Dani clasped the typewriter case firmly in her hand. She paid for the ticket and moved to the elevator. The operator waited for a full car before starting the switch. At each stop, her stomach rose and fell. Checking her watch again, she realized she was ten minutes early. Her thoughts turned to Alex. Well, he'll just have to get home on his own. I have more important things to do. Strolling nonchalantly to the elevator, she allowed her eyes to survey her surroundings. There was no sign of Valerie or Maria. Positioning herself opposite the exit to the observation deck, she stood quietly and waited. She wanted to see them before they saw her.

It was bright and clear. A brisk breeze lifted her hair and blew coolly against her cheek. She looked at the haze below and recalled the radio weather forecast this morning. The air quality was totally unacceptable. Dani wondered vaguely what the air was like in Argentina.

A group of tourists stepped closer to her, awed by the sight of the city below. The sun glinted on an airplane as it circled the building.

Dani watched the sleek, silvery jet as it started its descent.

'Look, Dad. An airplane!'

'I see it, son. They circle here before they descend to La Guardia and Kennedy.'

'Awk!' Dani squawked silently. Then the next wave of tourists emerged through the doors of the observation desk.

Dani blinked at Maria's bedraggled appearance. The youngster was walking beside a disheveled dark-haired woman. The child

291

started to run to Dani, only to be hindered by Valerie, clutching her back to her side.

Dani stared into the glittering eyes of the woman opposite her. She heard Maria squeal, 'Dani, it is me! You are not looking at me! Here I am!'

'I see you, honey,' Dani said, never taking her eyes from Valerie's hard face.

'Let's go to the upper observation deck. There are fewer tourists there, fewer prying eyes. You first, Miss Arnold.'

Minutes later, they emerged from the elevator into the small, round observation tower. Valerie was right. There was no one there. The sun streamed through the windows, making the room warm.

Valerie held Maria in a vise-like grip. 'Show me,' the desperate woman demanded.

Dani felt stunned as she stared at her glassy-eyed rival. She shook her head slightly. She couldn't go through with it.

'Now, or I'll twist her arm till it breaks,' Valerie hissed.

Dani gazed into the gleaming eyes, licked dry lips and slowly placed the case on the floor. Carefully, she withdrew the aged parchment.

Valerie made an involuntary move towards the case as she continued to clutch at the child.

Dani looked at her and felt a momentary

pang of pity as she watched the greed and hatred in her cold eyes.

Valerie stared down at the scrolls resting on the floor. She made no further move. Helplessness and despair washed over her countenance.

'They're only paper,' she tried a half-smile. 'Only paper. They never made Alex happy before. Only Maria has been able to do that.'

Valerie cast the child a puzzled, questioning look as though trying to measure her.

Dani watched Valerie's face transform from one of avarice to one of manic hatred. Fear clutched her throat.

'The last thing I want is to make Alex happy. No deal, Miss Arnold. Take your scrolls and go home.'

'But they'll get you. They'll find you. Alex will have Maria anyway.'

'No, he won't, Miss Arnold.' A mantle of determination settled over Valerie. 'No, he won't,' she said with authority.

Dani tried to quash the fear she felt for Maria. Malevolence shone in Valerie's eyes. A sadistic twitch pinched her upper lip.

Again, Dani looked into the angry eyes.

A low drown of an engine permeated the air within the tower. Maria tried to struggle from the woman's grasp. But Valerie held tighter, causing the young girl to cry out. Dani clenched her teeth, feeling strangled by a hard lump of terror in her throat. Imperceptibly, she moved toward the service stairs, anticipating Valerie's mad action to push Maria down them.

The droning became louder. Suddenly, Valerie stood transfixed, the sunlight streaming through the smoky windows behind her. She was looking off into the corner of the room.

'It's Brother Gian,' Maria whispered. At the sound of her daughter's words, Valerie backed up, slowly releasing her hold, all the while her gaze fixed on one corner of the building. Panic gripped her body making it hard to breathe. It couldn't be, not here in New York. Not that damn crazy monk. As though she were mounted on a spring, she jerked her eyes around, blank with fear. She made a move to clutch at the scrolls. Dani nimbly backed off a step holding Maria tightly to her side, sliding the scrolls with her foot, out of Valerie's reach.

A terrified scream at last found its escape from Valerie's gaping mouth. She stumbled toward the stairs as if trying to escape the ever-impending shadow. The pupils of Maria's eyes dilated with terror as she watched Valerie's crazed motions and heard her blood-curdling scream.

'Oh, my God!' Valerie screamed. 'Not me! I wasn't going to...' the words died in her throat.

Dani heard the heavy thud as Valerie lost her balance and tumbled down the stairs. Gently, Dani asked the child to stand by the wall. 'Stay here, Maria, don't move!'

'She saw the Monk, she saw Brother Gian ... I know that's what she saw,' Maria cried.

Dani grasped the girl by the shoulder, shaking her. 'Maria, stop this. Listen to me. What did you see? Tell me, what did you see?'

'Nothing, only my mother staring into a corner. She saw him! I saw, too. For the first time, my mother truly saw him.'

'Stay here, don't move from this spot!'

Before she touched the still body, Dani knew that Valerie was dead. She looked at the beautiful features of the woman and felt only pity.

Into the distance Dani looked at the small speck that was a plane. It was the two thirty. Could it really be?

'Oh, look at your beautiful apartment,' Maria cried, her eyes feverishly bright.

Dani cast an eye around the small apartment. Everything was blurred and out of focus. She no longer cared about it or anything else for that matter. The happenings of the afternoon had left her shaken and trembling.

'What time do you think Papa will be here?'

'Honey, I have no idea. I don't know if he'll come here or go to the house in the country. At this point, I don't know what we should do ourselves. I don't feel like making the trip back to the country. There's no reason why we can't stay here for the night. We could spread the blankets on the floor. What do you think?'

'It is fine with me. Dani, where did they ... I mean what happ ...Why can I not cry? Is there something wrong with me that will not allow me to cry? She was my mo—'

'Baby, I know how hard this must be for you but it was an accident. Don't ever for one minute think it was anything but an accident.'

'Who will tell my father?'

'I'll tell him when he comes here. Listen, sweetness, I have an idea,' Dani said with forced brightness. 'Why don't you go next door to Martha's and call for a pizza. Stash did a good job of cleaning up this mess but I want to vacuum before I put the blankets on the floor. This way, we'll both be busy.'

Maria obligingly trotted out to do Dani's bidding.

Lord, how was she to tell Alex? What would he say? Would he in some way blame her? She looked at her watch. He must have gone to the house in the country. Would he come here looking for them? It was five hours since his plane had landed. If he was coming, he would arrive shortly. Shaking her weary head, she perched on the arm of the broken club chair. It was over. Alex would take Maria and she would be alone again. God! After all this, the one thing she didn't want was to be all by herself.

The small apartment vacuumed, the girls sat chewing the stringy pizza. The doorbell rang and Maria cast an apprehensive glance in Dani's direction.

'You stay here, I'll get it,' Dani said, untangling herself from the mound of blankets on the floor.

'Who is it?'

'Alex.'

'It's your father,' Dani said softly as she slid the chain from the door. Maria nodded glumly.

Quickly and in a soft tone, Dani explained what had happened. Alex stared at Dani, his eyes cold and furious. 'What a waste of human life,' he said bitterly. 'There was no need for any of this.'

Dani motioned him to follow her into the empty living-room.

'Don't tell me that I am responsible for this also,' he said casting a narrowed eye around the barren room.

'It doesn't matter. I'm going away. The insurance company will take care of it. Alex,' Dani said quietly. 'You need to talk to Maria. Right now she needs you. I'll be in the kitchen.'

Dani fixed herself a cup of instant coffee and was leaning against the sink sipping it when Alex walked into the kitchen.

'I'm sorry I wasn't here. It must have been terrible for you.' He looked so dejected, so defeated, that Dani wanted to reach out and comfort him. Instead, she sipped at the scalding coffee.

'I'll survive. The question is, will Maria? She asked me why she couldn't cry. I didn't have the answer. Do you have the answer for your daughter, Alex?'

'No. There was a time when—'

Dani interrupted. 'The scrolls are in a case in the living-room.'

Alex nodded. 'I'll send Maria back to Argentina tomorrow. And you Dani, what about you?'

'I guess I'll leave. I think I'll take a plane and head for Aruba. I'll bask in the sun and—'

'And what?'

'I don't know. After my soul is warm, if that's possible, I'll decide.'

Alex's heart pounded at the vague words. 'I know this isn't the time to speak of my love for you but I must. You sound so ... far away,' he said hoarsely. 'I love you, Dani. I think I loved you the moment I saw you. If I seem cold and arrogant, as you say, it is only my defense against being ... hurt.' The

298

voice was humble in its entreaty. 'I decided on the way back from Rome to ask Valerie for a divorce. I want you for my wife, Dani. I ... I'll try to change.'

Dani felt faint stirrings in her heart, 'I'm not from your world, Alex. I don't think I could belong.'

'You're wrong. Don't you see, Querida, you are my world. For now, for tomorrow, for all time.' The warm Latin voice was husky with emotion. 'I need you, to be complete,' he said simply. 'Will you marry me? Before you answer, I must tell you that I am to return to Rome once more. Cardinal Palmerini wants me to bring the scrolls to him. I will return on the seventeenth of January. We could be married, if you agree, quietly, on the eighteenth. We could return together to the hacienda the following day.

'You're serious, aren't you?' Dani said in awe. 'I ... I...'

Maria peered in the door and laughed. 'Make her say "yes", Papa, then she cannot become a free spirit.'

'I thought I told you to stay out of my love life,' Dani said crossly. 'I'll make up my own mind if it's all right with you.'

'Very well,' the child said, withdrawing her head from the open doorway, 'as long as it is "yes" in the end.'

'It would seem that you are outnumbered,'

Alex smiled.

'It would seem so,' Dani said thoughtfully. 'But there is one flaw in your plan,' she uttered, sliding into the outstretched arms.

'Flaw! That is impossible. I allowed for any and all possibilities,' he said imperiously, as he crushed her slim body to his. 'Is it agreed?' he asked, laying his cheek against her dark head.

'I can't,' Dani said, rubbing her face against the rough material of his jacket. 'I have a date on the eighteenth that I wouldn't break for anything on this earth, my wedding included, but if you make it for the nineteenth, you have a date.'

Alex raised her face to meet his and brought his lips to hers. 'Forever and ever,' he murmured.

Maria smiled and clapped her hands as she withdrew from the doorway. Now Dani wouldn't be a free spirit.